Pride Publishing books by Samantha Cayto

Single Books
One Night in a Dungeon
Man Candy
Against a Rising Tide

Alien Slave Masters
The Captain's Pet
The Rebellious Pet
The Untamed Pet
The Captive Pet
The Inconvenient Pet
The Undercover Pet

Alien Blood Wars
Blood Dance
Dangerous Dance
Slave Dance
Star Dance
Mating Dance
Healing Dance
Smoke Dance
Final Dance: Part One
Final Dance: Part Two

Treaty Brides
Boi Bride
The Diplomat's Bride
Stolen Bride

Anthologies
His Rules: Safeword
Right Here, Right Now: Never the Groom

Collections
Rules of Summer: In the Heat of the Dungeon

Dark and Deadly: Dream Demon
S.W.A.L.K.: His True Heart
His Harem: Room for Elijah

Treaty Brides

STOLEN BRIDE

SAMANTHA CAYTO

Stolen Bride
ISBN # 978-1-80250-976-2
©Copyright Samantha Cayto 2022
Cover Art by Fiona Jayde ©Copyright August 2022
Interior text design by Claire Siemaszkiewicz
Pride Publishing

STOLEN BRIDE

Chapter One

"Drink up, your highness. You're falling behind."

Ronan, younger son of the king of Moorcondia, shot his companion the kind of prideful grin that he'd carefully cultivated since arriving at the university. "Alas, I have to leave for an assignation with a lady and can't afford to be too much in my cups." He slid the glass of beer back in the direction of his classmate.

The boy barked out a laugh and clapped Ronan on his shoulder with the kind of bone-jarring exuberance that seemed so common among boys of their age. Ronan didn't understand why every interaction had to turn into a contest of inflicting pain and humiliation. The others thought it all hilarious, reinforcing what he'd known for most of his life. He was not like them, not like any boy he'd ever met.

Not even his studious older brother thought anything strange about the rough and tumble lives of their male friends. It was merely that as the future ruler of their country, Morlen had the weight of duty on his shoulders and had to prepare for the time he would ascend to the throne. Such was the fate of the one of them who'd come out of the womb first, even by mere moments. He joined them when he could for nights of drinking and carousing, careful always not to do anything to tarnish his reputation. As the 'spare' in the family, Ronan had no expectations and could do most anything he liked. *No, not really.* He was only able to get away with what people thought a young, rich man would do. Too bad those were things he didn't like at all.

He didn't let his desires show on his face and instead bade his companions a good night. They gave him a raucous send-off, filled with innuendos of what they assumed he would get up to and demanding a full report the next day. He joined in the merriment with rehearsed bravado. "Now, lads, you know a gentleman never speaks of what happens between the sheets. I shall only say that I'm glad we don't have classes tomorrow."

Ronan threw on his heavy cloak and braced for the chilly night he knew waited for him outside. Spring was only grudgingly arriving, but his semester of classes would soon come to an end, and he could return to Moorcondia for the summer recess. It would be a relief to finally go home. This first year of university had proven more taxing than he'd expected. It wasn't his studies. It was the strain of keeping up his pretense of being a profligate rake. No one forced him to play this charade. Morlen certainly didn't care. But Ronan feared that if he didn't present the image of masculinity that everyone expected, they would easily see inside him, to his true self. He wasn't sure he could bear the scorn he felt certain would come his way.

I am a coward.

He considered, as he had many times, asking his parents to let him drop out. A university education was relatively new among the royal family. They might not care if he came back or not. But if he didn't, what would he do then? No matter how everyone had become accustomed to his uncle's new wife, Ronan wasn't so stupid as to assume his family and the members of court would accept him in any role other than an advisor to his brother. He would be expected to marry the proper noblewoman to add to the next generation of the family. That was his destiny, and staying at university helped put that eventuality off for a few years. There was value in that.

Ronan's personal guard, a somewhat grizzled man who was nonetheless capable of breaking a man's neck with a single twist, pushed away from the wall he'd been holding up in the drinking house and silently followed in Ronan's wake. He hated having to be chained to someone else all the time, but one older man who held no interest for him and kept his opinions to himself wasn't so bad, although the man's silent censure was often palpable. It was better than the contingent of younger guards who surrounded Morlen day and night—not that anyone really thought they were at risk here in this seat of learning… Still, it was important for the realm as well as each of them personally that they be safe from any violence. With Sir Frauk at his back, no one dared so much as shoot an angry look at him. Ronan simply had to pretend he didn't care about being shadowed by another who undoubtedly gave the king regular reports on how his younger son was running wild. His whole life had become one long effort at play-acting. It felt as if no one truly understood who and what he was, not even his twin.

Ronan tugged his cloak closer as he walked through the nearly empty streets of the old city, the sound of Sir Frauk's heavy-booted tread behind him. Monks had settled here long ago, attracting more people and founding a community. Starting a place of higher learning had come naturally to those original men, and now the university was surrounded by a vibrant city that existed on the edge of Moorcondia. It was a hub of trading, as well, attracting commerce from all over, except from those people who dwelled in the Dark Mountains. They kept to themselves, enigmas as much as the land where they lived. The craggy rocks were not inviting and rose high into the clouds.

They cast a looming shadow over this part of the city in particular — not surprising, given that this was where one went for less savory pursuits. The boys at the university considered it a badge of courage that they ventured here late at night. Ronan despised it and couldn't wait to reach his apartments. All he wanted to do was take a relaxing bath and curl up in bed with a good book. He could picture his valet waiting patiently for his return. Unlike Frauk, Igon was quick to show his disapproval of Ronan's nighttime pursuits. But once he'd settled Ronan into bed, he left him blessedly alone.

Ronan picked up his pace with eyes on the uneven cobblestones to ensure that he didn't slip. The fashionable boots he wore pleased him, but they weren't very sturdy. The last thing he wanted was for Frauk to think it was drink that made him stumble. The man suddenly uttered a muted cry, very unlike him. Ronan turned to see why and froze at the sight of the large soldier crashing to the ground. Another man, little more than a dark figure, heavily armed, loomed over him. Ronan stepped forward, although to do what he couldn't fathom. He was terrible at the martial arts and didn't possess so much as knife on him.

A rush of air and a flicker of something out of the corner of his eye was all the warning he got before someone grabbed him from behind. He was swept off his feet, and a cloth was pressed against his nose and mouth. Trained in warfare as he was, he instinctively started to put up a fight. Whoever had him, though, was far stronger, the man's massive arm holding him around his chest in a vise-like grip. And there was something soaking the gag, a sweet smell that made his head swim. As he fought to regain his freedom, the drug caused his muscles to go lax. Then there was nothing.

* * * *

Ronan came to with a pounding headache and a thick tongue. It took him a moment or two to assess his situation. It was night still, only now he was among the trees of a dense forest, not the stone buildings of the city. And he was on horseback, the gentle swaying of such a beast well-known to him. But he wasn't riding so much as being carried astride. His head and back were propped against a hard, yet warm, wall. He might have drifted back to sleep due to the rather pleasant location, except the circumstances of his attack came to him in a flash. Popping open his eyes farther, he struggled to gain freedom.

An arm that had lain loosely against his waist tightened. "Easy, your highness. I have you securely on my mount."

Those were not comforting words, given the situation, and they were uttered with an accent that was unfamiliar to him. They rumbled through the broad chest against which he was being held. He tried to claw that arm away, but covered as it was in thick leather bands, he had no impact. It was while he did so that he noticed there were others riding around them, slipping in and out of his field of vision among the trees. To a man they were large, imposing figures dressed in dark clothing. They reminded him of the evil specters he'd seen illustrated in one of his favorite books. He wasn't so fanciful, however, as to believe them to be anything other than men who wished him harm, so he opened his mouth to yell for help.

His captor's hand clapped across his lips before he could utter a sound. "We have not yet cleared the outer farms of the city. If you scream, men may come running to your rescue, and we'll be forced to kill them. I don't want that. Do you?"

There was something about the man's tone that skittered up Ronan's spine and made him shudder. It wasn't fear, although that was there in abundance. It was a different kind of emotional reaction that nevertheless frightened him, too. He shook his head, because the man seemed to be waiting for a reply, and of course, the last thing Ronan wanted was for his father's subjects to die in vain on his behalf.

"Good. Now do I have your word that if I remove my hand, you won't cry out?"

Galling as it was, Ronan nodded, and when his mouth was liberated, he kept his promise. That didn't mean he would stay silent. He tried to turn to look at his captor. "What do you think you are doing?"

The man stared down at him, his broad, close-bearded face partially concealed by the nose plate of his helmet. "Kidnapping you."

Ronan huffed in indignation. "I am aware of *that*. Why? What do you want from me?"

"From you, nothing much."

"You must be seeking money. I have access to plenty of coin if you take me back to the city." Surely that was all it would take for this nightmare to end.

"I don't want your money." The infuriating man spoke as if they discussed the weather and not Ronan's fate, whatever that might be.

Reaching inside his shirt, Ronan pulled out the simple, yet very valuable, dark sapphire pendant his mother had given him on his eighteenth birthday. Morlen had received one exactly like it, masculine and beautiful at the same time. "If not that, what about this? Take it and leave me to find my way back." He knew there was a flaw to his logic. The man could yank the necklace from Ronan's neck and still hold him for ransom. Perhaps the guy and his cohorts weren't very bright.

The man huffed what might have been a laugh. "Your trinket doesn't interest me in the least."

That answer stunned Ronan into silence. The pendant was very valuable, he was sure. His mother would never give her sons anything less. Nothing about this misadventure made any sense. And as they traveled deeper into unknown territory, Ronan had to work to suppress his growing fear.

"Then tell me what you want!" He was careful to keep his voice down but couldn't hide his emotions, never could.

"It is complicated. Here and now is not the time or place to explain. We'll make camp for a short while once we have crossed the Moorcondian border. For now, you need do nothing more than rest, if that is your wont. As I said, I have you securely on my steed." There was silence for the space of a few horse steps, then, "I won't let anything bad happen to you."

As ridiculous as that reassurance was, it nevertheless sent something like relief coursing through Ronan. Encircled in the man's powerful arms, he perversely did feel safe, if one didn't count the danger the man himself presented. "You mean other than being knocked unconscious by some drug and stolen away by brigands for the gods know what reason?"

There was a pause. "Yes, other than that. And I don't know about your gods, but the All Mother understands what is at stake and sees what is in my heart. This is necessary."

"So you say." Ronan couldn't help fuming. Another thought popped into his aching head. "What of Sir Frauk? You killed *him*." While he'd resented the man's presence, he hated the idea that he'd died trying to save him.

"We did no such thing. He was knocked out, tied up and we even found a reasonably warm place for him to remain until he wakes."

"You're lying." Ronan knew brigands, especially those who ransomed wealthy people, had no scruples.

"Why would I bother to do so? You are already furious, yet well within my control. There would be no benefit to lying about the fate of your man."

Ronan had to admit to himself that there was some logic in what his captor said. He kept that observation to himself, however, and said no more. His head still ached, and he was exhausted. There was nothing he could do to free himself at the moment. The only option open to him was to bide his time and hope for a chance at escape. He tried to keep himself upright instead of leaning against his abductor, but his fatigue mixed with the gentle rhythm of the horse's movement made that impossible. As hard as the man's chest was, it made for a decent resting place. Ronan couldn't keep his eyes open.

"Who are you, anyway?" he managed to ask in a sleepy voice.

"I am Jarl Tarben of the Dark Mountains."

That information intrigued Ronan as much as it alarmed him. He'd never before met anyone from that mysterious and isolated country. But as the man had called him 'your highness' he undoubtedly knew the prize he possessed. With the last of his strength, Ronan used that identity as a warning. "I am Ronan, prince of Moorcondia. My father the king will have your head for this."

The man sighed silently, only the movement of his chest telling the tale. "Well, he can try."

Ronan made an effort to rally with a retort, but he was too tired to do so. Besides, even as he issued the threat, he wasn't sure he wanted that outcome.

* * * *

Tarben glanced down at the top of his captive's sleeping head. He knew that the foul stuff he'd used to knock the boy out was to blame, but also understood that it was easier to find solace in sleep than to face the fear of what was to become of him. While Tarben knew that he would keep the prince safe, there was no way for the boy to know that. It would take time to prove it through actions, although matters between them would get worse—far worse—before they got better. *If they ever do.*

The idea of being tied to someone who loathed him for the rest of his life was unpleasant, to say the least. Not that there was a choice. His duty to the people of the Dark Mountains took precedence over all other considerations, including his own happiness. He might not be his sire's heir, but he was still bound by the obligations of being the man's son. The distasteful act of kidnapping the Moorcondian prince was necessary, the last, best hope his people had. He would do this, as there was no choice. All he could hope was that he could make a decent life for the boy slumped against him.

It wouldn't be any kind of hardship for him. The slender form resting against his chest stirred strong feelings in him. There was the urge to protect someone smaller and weaker, that was true enough. His reaction was more than that, though. Prince Ronan was the type of man who had always appealed to Tarben. He liked someone lithe in his bed who fit easily against his shoulder. A small, tight rump was a particular weakness of his. Just the feel of it pressed against his groin was sufficient to make him hard, even with the layers of thick clothing between them. And thank the All Mother for that. The last thing he wanted was to add to the lad's fright by prodding him with a stiff cock. Tarben would never impose that part of himself on anyone. It was the single thing he could control in this whole miserable affair. When he'd made that silent vow to himself, he hadn't counted on being as attracted to the Moorcondian prince as he was. Living a chaste life wasn't an appealing vision of his future, but such was the price of privilege — for both of them. They were second sons and duty-bound to play their roles in unexpected ways.

The slow passage through the dark forest made it easy for him to get lost in his thoughts. It was a monotonous journey, although knowing he was nearly at the border with his own country bettered his mood. There was no one following them. Those of his men whose job it was to protect their back and wipe their trails as much as possible would cry out a warning if that changed. The rest of the soldiers ranged around them, a quiet escort that showed as familiar shadows in the gloom. He knew that he — and by extension Ronan — were as safe as they could be. These were Tarben's hand-picked men, those he trusted the most out of all his father's force of fighters. Once they crossed the narrow river that hugged the border, they would meet up with the others. His father and the cousin who advised him had insisted on a larger contingent, just in case the Moorcondians had more palace guards watching over the prince than was known.

Normally Tarben would be suspicious of the ease with which the prince had been snatched, but in this case, he was confident that no such back-up had existed. Apparently, King Auden was unconcerned for his second's son's safety, perhaps because it was obvious that this boy would never be a fighter and therefore not worthy of anyone else's attention. Or it might simply be that the man was as heartless about his own child as he was about the plight of his Dark Mountains neighbors.

The sound of rushing water reached his ears, sending a small amount of relief through him. Once they had crossed the river, they would be in friendly territory that he and his men knew like the backs of their hands. But they had not reached safety yet and needed to remain vigilant for trouble, even a naturally occurring one. Early spring thawing from the mountains fed the river, making it icy cold and treacherously fast. He wasn't overly worried, because they'd traveled from here a scant day ago and had crossed without mishap. Their warhorses were sturdy and sure-footed beasts. Nevertheless, he watched how well his vanguard maneuvered the crossing before moving forward to do the same. As he approached the slippery bank, he tightened his grip on his passenger, surprisingly concerned about making sure he didn't slip off. That effort in turn caused the boy to rouse.

"What's happening?"

Tarben hated the alarm in his captive's voice. "Easy, boy. We are crossing the river that boarders our two countries. Once on the other side, you will be in the Kingdom of the Dark Mountains." His reassurances fell on deaf ears. Ronan grabbed hold of Tarben's arm and tried to twist to look behind them. The sudden movement caused the horse to become skittish. Tarben easily brought it back under control before admonishing the prince more harshly than he'd intended.

"Be still! If you fall into the water, I will be forced to jump in after you, and I don't relish freezing my balls off. There is no one coming to your rescue, in any event," he added more kindly. "You are mine now." He hadn't intended to be so possessive, yet his own words caused something to well up deep inside him.

Prince Ronan didn't give him a chance to dwell on that, however. He squirmed in Tarben's hold a bit before settling down with a noticeable shudder. "What are you going to do to me?" There were tears showing in his voice.

Tarben had to harden his heart, even as he sought to soothe the boy. "I won't hurt you, but you and I are both insignificant parts of a serious game that can mean the difference between life and death for thousands. I told you I would explain matters later. We are nearly at the point at which we can rest for a while."

His captive didn't fight him anymore, simply sat with his back straight so as not to lean against Tarben's chest. He missed the contact, although he was hardly in a position to complain. He was not the aggrieved party in this drama. As soon as his horse's hooves clomped in the mud on the other side, his father's waiting warriors appeared at the tree line to greet them. The prince gasped and actually shrank against Tarben now. It would have been delightful if not born of fear.

"Those are my men. They intend you no harm."

"As if you and I have the same definition of what that means," the prince sneered.

That small show of defiance pleased Tarben. The Moorcondian appeared delicate, but he wasn't weak or cowed. Tarben sought a different way to reassure him. "I shall be the only man to touch you from this point forward."

"Is that supposed to bring me comfort?"

"It is all I have to give." It saddened Tarben that it was true.

He rode into the middle of the makeshift camp his men had formed and stopped his horse near the fire in the middle. One of the soldiers came to take hold of the horse's reins to make it easier for Tarben to dismount. He did so, keeping one hand on Ronan and the other on the saddle, then he pulled his captive off and set him on his feet. The boy didn't fight him, but his knees started to buckle as soon as Tarben tried to release him. Instead, he took a firmer grip, this time around his waist, and led him away from the horse and over to the fire. His men stared at the Moorcondian prince with open curiosity and, for some, hostility. Tarben used his own glare to remind them they were to show his captive the respect his station deserved.

"Here, you will bed down by the fire for warmth."

The prince dug in his heels. "I need to relieve myself."

"Of course." Tarben did as well, now that it had been mentioned. "I'll take you to a place of privacy."

There was little to be had of that in a soldiers' encampment, and no one cared about exposing themselves in such situations anyway. Ronan was different—in Tarben's view at least. The boy deserved to be sheltered from prying eyes—all those except Tarben's, that was. He led Ronan to a spot behind a big tree and let him go as soon as he was sure the boy could stand on his own. Sweeping aside the apron of his leather breastplate, he plucked at the laces of his breeches while keeping an eye on his captive.

Ronan grimaced. "Must you stand so close?"

"Alas, I must. I can tell you are weighing the idea of bolting for freedom. I need to be able to stop that nonsense before it happens."

The boy shot him a look of pure hatred. "You think me silly for trying to regain my freedom?"

"I do when it means running through an unknown forest with many dangers lurking. Even if you don't risk drowning by trying to cross the river, there are wild beasts, including men, who would bring an end to you before you even knew that you were under attack. I must keep you safe from that."

The prince looked away on a huff and eventually managed to relieve himself, even with Tarben so close. Tarben had no difficulty, naturally, and waited patiently, giving as much privacy as he could until the boy was done. He led him back to the camp, not quite holding on to him, but with his hand hovering near, just in case it became necessary. Desperate people, like animals, couldn't be trusted to act rationally. Once they reached the fire, Tarben waved at the fur pallet laid down for their comfort. "Here's where we spend the rest of the night. I'll have water and some food brought first."

Instead of sitting, the prince crossed his arms and glared at him mulishly. "You said you'd tell me what this is all about. I want to know now what you are going to do with me."

Understanding that the time had come to explain their unusual fate, Tarben steeled himself for the virulent, possibly violent, reaction he was going to get. He looked the boy straight in the eyes as he answered. "I'm going to marry you."

Chapter Two

"Drink this."

Ronan shot his kidnapper and soon-to-be rapist what he hoped was a look of defiance. It was all an act, of course, intended to hide the fact that he was fighting back tears. He very much worried that he wasn't pulling it off, but he was a prince after all and had some pride. He had to at least try. Plus, he felt like a fawn surrounded by wolves. If his fate was sealed, the least he could do was go down with his head held high. The urge to bat the flask away was strong, yet he resisted. He had to be smart, if nothing else, and fighting a losing battle would only deplete what strength he had.

Grabbing the flask, he first sniffed, then took a tentative sip. When it proved to be nothing more than water, he drank greedily. What beer he'd had at the pub, coupled with the drug he'd been forced to inhale, had left him very thirsty. He couldn't afford to become dehydrated. If a chance to escape presented itself, he needed to be capable of quick action. He was hungry, too, yet held his tongue on that problem. He wouldn't give this Dark Mountains man the satisfaction of asking for food. As with the water, it would likely be offered at some point. He was no good as a captive if he succumbed to something preventable like hunger. It was hard to tell how clever this Jarl Tarben was, but the man had proved solicitous of Ronan's needs so far—not that such behavior counted for anything, given the kidnapping and what was threatened to come. The man was a monster, and Ronan couldn't lose sight of that fact.

"Here. It's not much but will sustain you until we can obtain fresh kills."

Ronan eyed the strip of dried meat. Many of the people at court would turn their noses up at such basic fare. He wasn't one of them. The excess at meals bothered his stomach. A slice of bread with cheese and beef sufficed when he was given the choice. He took the offering without comment, bit off a chunk and chewed, not caring about his manners. Tarben squatted beside him, his feet just beyond the pelt on which Ronan sat. While the man obviously was careful not to get too close, his proximity was disturbing, nevertheless. Ronan made a point of turning his body away from him.

There was a quick, low sound, part sigh, part grumble. "When you are finished, lie down for some sleep. We can afford to tarry a while, but at dawn, we must leave."

Ronan ate more dried meat and washed it down with the water. While he understood that any delay might increase the chance of their being found by a contingent of his father's men, he wasn't sure it was fair to even hope for such a thing. There were perhaps a mere two dozen of the Dark Mountains warriors surrounding him. The soldiers garrisoned in the university city were ten-fold that number. But they existed mostly to keep the peace. Handling thieves and the odd murderer was the most fighting they saw.

Tarben's men were large and bore themselves with the kind of powerful confidence that he expected was battle-honed. They were heavily armed as well, carrying large swords on their belts, while a few also had crossbows slung over their backs. These men weren't resting, regardless of having made camp. They were ready for a fight, and he feared that his father's soldiers would be cut down quickly. He didn't want their deaths on his conscience. It would be better to give his father and uncle time to mount a strong military campaign to rescue him. He would suffer in the meantime but survive. It was the kind of price one had to pay for the sake of the Moorcondian people when one was a member of the royal family.

He swallowed the last bite of food and lifted his chin as he stared at his captor. "I don't need to sleep. I did plenty of that on the journey here." His cheeks warmed at the memory of how he'd rested against his abductor. He shouldn't have slept so soundly under the circumstances. *It was the drug, that's all.*

Tarben scrutinized him long enough that Ronan worried his thoughts showed on his face. "A fair point," the man finally said. "I promised you an explanation, however, and I will give it to you before we break camp."

Ronan turned his head away because now he was sure his cheeks were red. "What you said is ridiculous. I won't marry you."

"There is no choice in that—for either of us."

"Huh! I don't see a knife at *your* throat."

Tarben was silent for a moment after that. "You're wrong." His voice was softer than usual and filled with some kind of emotion. "Like you, I am the son of a king and duty-bound to do what is best for my people."

Ronan hated hearing the echo of his thoughts, so he swiveled his head to glare at the man. "How is kidnapping and forcing me into marriage helping them?"

"With you tied to me, it will force your father to negotiate a treaty."

Ronan gasped at the answer. "That is what this is all about? Good gods, are you Dark Mountains people so backward that you don't even understand how to approach a neighboring country for diplomacy?" He wanted to laugh at the absurdity of it all, except that Tarben's expression was starkly serious.

"We may have isolated ourselves for many generations, but we are not ignorant savages."

"Really?" Ronan patted his own chest. "I think I'm proof of how much of a lie that is." He held the man's gaze, although he braced for a blow, because he could see the anger in the man's eyes.

None came. Instead, Tarben banked his feelings and answered with a stern, yet measured tone. "This is the end product of our efforts at diplomacy with your king. We *started* with multiple requests for a meeting to discuss matters. My cousin, acting as the king's advisor, sent envoys last spring and made attempts thereafter as well. We were rebuffed each time. Your king refused to even hear us out."

Temporarily stunned at this news, Ronan could only sit and blink at his captor for a few moments before saying, "That's not how my father rules."

Tarben lifted his eyebrows. "How would you know? You are the pampered second son who spends his time at useless lessons, drinking, gambling and carousing. I doubt thoughts about the governance of your country have ever entered your pretty head."

Ronan was outraged at the comment, even though he was the one responsible for cultivating his own reprobate image. It was the only way he knew how to hide who he really was. His façade might cause heads to shake, but his true self would only invite scorn. He let some of his feelings show before wiping them from his expression, but only the fury and resentment had been aired for the Dark Mountains warrior. The fact that part of him was stupidly happy at the idea his captor thought him pretty was something too shameful to see the light of day.

"I know my father. He's not one to dismiss someone without at least hearing them out."

"And yet, here we are because he did exactly that." Tarben glanced at his men. "Break camp." Not even waiting to see that his order was being carried out, he turned his attention back to Ronan. "There is an abbey that we will reach just before darkness falls again. There we will be wed."

"I told you I will *not* marry you." Surely that was one area that he had some control over. No one could make him pledge himself to this man, even under threat of death. Ronan might be different from other boys, but he was not a coward, even if he was scared witless.

"We will be bound together, nevertheless. Your compliance is not required."

Ronan crossed his arms. "How barbaric."

"I don't think a Moorcondian can take the moral high ground on this matter. Ask the Duchess of Vostguard if you disagree."

Damn, he had a point, except... "My uncle's wife was forced into marriage by his own people, not mine."

Tarben nodded. "True and likewise, I act under the command of my king. And while it is I who force you, I do so in order to ensure that your father does not rebuff our efforts at a treaty. And," he added with a heavy breath, "your being my wife will ensure that whatever treaty we do make will be honored."

It took a moment for the meaning of the man's words to sink in. Ronan couldn't hold back his gasp. "You mean to keep me here in the Dark Mountains for the rest of my life? I will never go home again or see my family?" It hadn't been obvious to him what this talk of marriage had really meant. Now the tears did flow. He couldn't hold them back or hide his misery. "You can't do that to me," he added, finding it hard to take a breath.

"I'm sorry. I can't tell you for a certainty what the future will hold. However, I can promise I will permit you to visit your family when it is safe under the treaty to do so."

"*Permit*?" Outrage overtook the tears, and when Tarben tried to put his hand on Ronan's shoulder, he slapped it away. "Don't touch me."

"That demand is going to be impossible to satisfy." The man sounded weary and looked it too as he rose to his feet. "We're leaving now."

When he reached for him again, Ronan fought in earnest, with arms flailing and legs kicking. The outcome of the battle was pre-ordained, naturally. He'd never excelled at fighting skills and the difference in their strength allowed Tarben to easily pick him up and haul him over to the horse. The Dark Mountains men watched the show with mostly passive faces, although one or two openly smirked at his plight. Matters didn't improve any when Tarben had one particularly sober-looking man bind Ronan's hands loosely in front of him.

"I cannot risk your hurting my horse," was Tarben's explanation before he tossed Ronan onto the beast.

At least he sat astride instead of being slung over the saddle on his stomach. And when Tarben joined him, the man's arm encircled his waist once more to hold him steady. When they rode out of the camp, Ronan could only try to keep from crying and shaking as he headed for his hideous fate.

* * * *

Tarben had always been a simple man in many ways. He worked hard, did his duty and banked his anger over matters he couldn't control. As he approached the wide gates of Sentinel Abbey, however, he let himself acknowledge every bit of resentment he felt toward the Moorcondian king, his own and even the All Mother for the predicament he was in and for the ignoble act he was about to commit. With each clomp of his horse's hooves, another piece of his honor was stripped away as he prepared to brutalize his captive, in spirit if not in body.

The boy sat limply in his embrace, his tears and fight having evaporated at some point during their long ride. Tarben wanted nothing more than to gather him close and soothe away his fright, but his advances would not be welcome and his efforts rather disingenuous. *I can't make this any less awful for him.* Or for himself, except that didn't signify. He'd never intended to marry a woman, so tying himself to the Moorcondian prince didn't upend his life. Nor could he pretend that the idea of having this boy in his bed was a hardship. No, the problem was that they could easily live the rest of their lives lying chastely side-by-side, each miserable in their own ways.

They came to a stop at the gates. He'd sent his most trusted warrior, Alf, as the point man. Alf dismounted and rang the bell set into a recessed part of the imposing stone wall while the rest of them waited, horses and men alike tired from the long journey that had started days ago and with little sleep. If the reverend mother was in a good mood, she might permit them to make camp within the Abbey's walls. When no one came to greet them, Alf rang the bell again. It was cold enough that one could see the horses' breath. A shiver ran through Ronan and Tarben instinctively tried to hold him closer for warmth. Of course, he was rebuffed.

Finally a nun came out of the abbey, her black robes billowing out behind her as she hurried to greet them. She stopped just beyond the gates and assessed them with a keen eye. Her gaze swept them all, lingering on Tarben and his captive, as she waited for them to explain themselves.

"Jarl Tarben has urgent business with the reverend mother," Alf pronounced.

The nun didn't move. "Do you bring trouble to this abbey, Jarl?" She directed her question to Tarben.

"No." As the son of a king, he'd learned to express himself emphatically and with no more explanation that was necessary. And he spoke the truth. Even if the

Moorcondians risked their prince's life by invading the Dark Mountains, nothing of what he'd learned of them made him fear that they would sack an abbey unless it housed the person they sought. Tarben wouldn't linger longer than a day there.

"Very well." The nun unlocked the gates with a large key that was chained to her waist and left them to find their own way in.

Alf and another man swung the gates open so that they could all ride through. As they entered the courtyard, Ronan shifted and his body stiffened. He asked no questions and didn't need to. The boy was not so foolish as to not recognize that this was a holy place and that their marriage would take place here. When Tarben reined in his horse and dismounted, his bride-to-be began to struggle. There was no contest. Tarben had no trouble yanking him down and setting him on his feet. It was easy, as well, to hold him tight and drag him toward the abbey's front doors. Those men who were his most trusted companions looked away, hiding their disgust at this necessary barbarity. The Dark Mountains people were strong and fearless, but not overtly cruel. It would have disappointed him if his men had found nothing wrong with what he did. Some of the others among them, however — the ones he hadn't chosen himself — appeared to almost enjoy the spectacle. Tarben made a mental note to instill upon them that they'd better treat his bride with respect.

He wrangled Ronan up the steps and through the open doors. They led directly into the abbey's ancient chapel. It was the oldest house of worship in their country. He'd been there a few times in his life, and he was struck anew by the majesty of its soaring ceiling and intricate wood carvings. He hated to sully this place with his actions, but there was no choice and what needed to be done would best be done quickly. He dragged the ever-more-struggling Ronan down the aisle. The reverend mother stood at the end, ready to greet them, her face its usual inscrutable self. The woman was almost as old as time and had run this abbey for a very long while. She was as shrewd as she was devoted to the All Mother. He knew he could count on her agreeing to his request.

"Reverend Mother." He bowed his head. "I have need of a marriage."

The woman perused them, taking in the Moorcondian prince with narrowed eyes. "An unusual request from two men."

"But not prohibited." In this he was sure, because his father's legal advisor had scoured her texts before giving the advice that the plan could work. It seemed that no one in the known world had thought to lay out such specificity in who could be wed.

The reverend mother considered it briefly, the wheels in her head almost visible as they whirled around, weighing the costs and benefits of performing the ceremony. "I suppose that is true. The All Mother in her infinite wisdom and mercy would not deny the union of any two people of proper age who wish it."

Ronan kicked at Tarben as his struggles increased. "No! I don't—"

Tarben clamped his hand over the boy's mouth. "We're in something of a hurry, I'm afraid. Might we impose upon you at this very moment?"

The woman looked down her nose at them, her expression harsh and her eyes still narrowed, an impressive feat of hers, given that she wasn't nearly as tall as he was. Her gaze flicked from Ronan's muffled mouth to Tarben's face. He saw her objection and had anticipated it. Here was where her practicality could be leveraged to override her scruples.

Tarben turned his head to give a silent command to Alf. "We appreciate how inconvenient our request is. Please accept this modest contribution from my father, the king, to the abbey's upkeep."

Alf presented the woman with a purse heavy with an amount of coin that no one could afford to refuse. It was a necessary sacrifice, given how much would be gained if this scheme proved successful. *Please, All Mother, let it be so.* There was nothing to guarantee that the Moorcondian king would care enough about his second son to agree to anything. The intelligence they had gathered indicated that the man was devoted to his family in general. This venture would prove the truth of that belief. If they were wrong in their assumptions, Tarben and Ronan would be doubly screwed.

The reverend mother merely glanced at the purse before waving toward a nun beside her. Alf handed over the bribe, and both he and the nun faded out of sight. What was about to happen needed to be witnessed by others, but it was still a private affair between the couple and the All Mother. The reverend mother merely acted as a necessary conduit to bind the covenant he and Ronan were about to make with the deity. Tarben knew without being told to go kneel at the woman's feet. It was difficult to get Ronan into position, but once he did, the ceremony began. It didn't take long before he and the Moorcondian prince were bound together in holy matrimony for the rest of their lives.

* * * *

Ronan sat cross-legged on the pallet in the small room that the woman who ruled this abbey had allocated to him and Tarben for the night. It was sparse and cold, with only one wall-mounted lamp to give it any light, because there was no window. He supposed a pious person living in the abbey would be content with it. For him, it was nothing more than a cell in which he was locked. Although he could open the door, one of Tarben's men stood guard outside. The man was as big as the mountains for which his country was named. There was no way to get past him. Of Tarben, he'd seen nothing since he'd escorted his new 'bride' to this place, which was all to the good given what was going to happen once the man did arrive.

It was funny how he'd envisioned for a long time what it would be like to be swept into a man's arms and made love to. He'd pleasured himself at the thought as much as his imagination allowed. Now that the reality was here, it made him sick to his stomach. He'd only managed to pick at the rather meager meal a smiling nun had brought to him earlier. Its remains sat on a plate in one corner, along with a bowl of water and a cloth. He had no interest in cleaning himself for his abductor's pleasure. Because he had no sense of time in this place, he wasn't sure if it was meant to be a late midday meal or an early supper. Either way, Jarl Tarben would come to him soon, he was sure. Why wouldn't the man? He had someone waiting for him upon whom he could slake his lust. Ronan shuddered at the notion, and he hugged himself for a small amount of comfort. There was no way he could fight the man.

When the door suddenly opened, he scrambled into the corner as far as he could go. Tarben came in, and the sight of him derailed Ronan's fear for a little while. The man looked so different. Gone was the battle helmet, giving Ronan a clear view of his face for the first time. It was quite handsome for all its fierceness, and his hair hung down in freshly washed waves to his massive shoulders. Every bit of the man's strength was open for observation, despite his loose-fitting tunic and trousers. There were no weapons to be seen. *Not surprising.* He didn't need any to subdue Ronan, and why risk them being turned on him? Ronan had half hoped that he would have that opportunity, although whether he would really try to kill Tarben or not was unknown. It would mean his own death, and surely living was better, no matter what. So long as he survived his ordeal, he had a chance of being rescued.

Tarben frowned at the sight of the barely touched meal. "You didn't eat."

"I wasn't hungry."

Tarben was clearly displeased, but he merely picked up the plate and handed it to the guard outside. "The jarlina is done with this. See that it doesn't go to waste." He shut the door again and stood staring at Ronan. "We'll leave the water. You might want the use of it later."

Ronan's stomach lurched at the implication. "After you defile me, you mean." Tarben opened his mouth. Ronan rolled over him. "What did you refer to me as just now? I am *Prince Ronan.*"

"In Moorcondia, yes. Here you are Jarlina Tarben. An unusual official style for a man, I'll grant you, but we have no other point of reference. You are the wife of a jarl and therefore, carry the feminine version of my title under our law. For better or worse, your identity is tied to mine."

Ronan balled his hands into fists. "I am not your property."

'No one said you were."

"I'm not your *wife*, either." Ronan put as much venom in his voice as he could.

"There, I have to disagree." Tarben sat on the floor and started taking off his boots. "We are married, Ronan. That is fact."

Suppressing his fear, Ronan argued the point. "I said no vows."

"We don't here." The man set one boot aside before starting on the other. "Marriage is a covenant between the couple and the All Mother, facilitated by the officiant. In this case, that was Reverend Mother Mauve. There is nothing for us to say because we asked for the union the moment we knelt at the altar. Everything after that was the blessing of the All Mother and her admonishment that we live our lives true to her as a married couple."

"I don't believe in your All Mother." He'd never heard of such a thing. There were many gods, some of whom took on a female aspect, but not this overarching female the Dark Mountain people seemed to worship.

Tarben put his second boot with the first and sat cross-legged, much as Ronan did, albeit more at ease. "It doesn't matter. Either she exists or not." He shrugged his shoulders. "This is a matter of my people's law, and in that, we are married."

Ronan didn't bother to respond to that point. It was hard to even form a thought through his growing fear. As disheveled and smelly as he must be from his ordeal, Tarben clearly wanted him. The loose trousers were tented by his erect cock. The sight of it made Ronan's own dick and balls shrivel in response. There was nothing enticing about being with a man under these circumstances. He was a prince, however, and he pulled out his pride.

"I will not give myself to you freely. You'll have to take me by force."

Tarben looked more sad than disappointed. "I understand your feelings on the matter. And I will not take you against your will."

A rush of relief made him almost dizzy before he saw the trap. "That's a lie. You have to consummate the marriage for it to be valid. Your entire scheme depends on it. You might not use outright violence, but you will try to pleasure me to give the illusion of consent."

"Good Mother!" Tarben's eyes went wide for a second. "I will do no such thing. I understand you have no reason to believe this, but I am a man of honor."

Ronan couldn't help snorting. "Yes, that *is* hard to believe, not that it matters. Your whole plan only works if we are truly married in a way my father cannot annul — other than by having your head cleaved from your body, that is. You have no choice in deflowering me." He winced inwardly at the stark admission. With his friends, he pretended that he'd bedded many women. The truth was, he'd known no touch other than his own.

"What you say may be true in your country, but not here. Sex is not a requirement to bind a marriage. The abbey has recorded our union that was witnessed by warriors and nuns alike. Our legal joining stands, no matter what we do or don't do on this pallet."

Ronan couldn't trust those words, and he felt strangely conflicted about them for a moment or two before reminding himself that rape wasn't something to desire. "If that is true, then you will sleep elsewhere."

Tarben shook his head. "No. It is my right to at least bed down by your side, and that pallet will be more comfortable than the ground my men are camped out on. A good night's sleep will be welcome. We have many days' journey to reach my father's castle." With that, Tarben moved over to lie down on the pallet. The man's large body left little room for Ronan, who still cowered in the corner.

"Do you intend to remain upright for the entire night?"

"No." Ronan laid himself out from pride alone. He didn't want this man to see any more of his fear. There was room, but their bodies touched here and there. "This isn't comfortable."

Tarben rolled onto his side away from him. "Better?"

"Yes." Ronan did have more room but also perversely missed the warm contact. "You won't touch me?"

"Not unless you ask me to."

"That will never happen."

"Unfortunate, yet your prerogative. Now go to sleep, wife."

Ronan bit back a retort about how he was no such thing and he'd sleep when he wanted, not when commanded. Yet, the defiance ran out of him, and soon he couldn't do anything other than obey.

Chapter Three

"Let me help you."

Ronan slapped away the proffered hand. "I can mount a horse on my own."

There was no admonishment from his so-called husband. Tarben simply stepped back, and Ronan hauled himself onto the saddle of the man's large steed. It was no easy feat, but he landed astride and sat still while Tarben mounted behind him and reached around to take the reins. Ronan tried to keep their bodies from touching, but he wasn't in control of the situation. As before, Tarben encircled Ronan's waist with one arm, holding Ronan close. He was forced to accept what Tarben did with as little reaction as he could manage. There was no way he wanted any of these Dark Mountains men to see how scared he still was. And that was despite the chaste night he'd spent with Tarben.

True to his word, the man hadn't forced him or even tried to seduce him. There had been no overt effort to make contact, at least by Tarben. It caused Ronan's cheeks to heat, however, when he remembered waking pressed against Tarben's larger, warmer body. In his sleep, he'd gravitated toward the man, who had given him an infuriatingly smug look when he'd woken to find Ronan snuggled up to him. More disconcertingly, they'd both been hard when they rose. Although Tarben hadn't said anything to point out Ronan's obvious arousal, there had been more of that smugness.

Ronan had told himself — and was still doing so — that his dick was a mindless piece of flesh reacting to the proximity of a desirable man. It couldn't reason out how intolerable the situation was, and Ronan's only hope was that somehow this terrible event would end with his return to Moorcondia. Whatever the rules were in the Dark Mountains, he held on to the fact that his country wouldn't recognize a marriage that was challenged on grounds of lack of consummation. So long as he held firm against the temptation, he had reason for hope. That was assuming, of course, that Tarben didn't lie about their relationship. There was no way to prove consummation either way, even for women. Witnesses were relied upon, and all of those were Tarben's men.

No. He wasn't going to worry about that, if for no other reason than the jarl seemed to be, at his core, an honorable man — the kidnapping and forced marriage notwithstanding. It was hard to imagine many other men in Tarben's position not pressing for what they saw as their conjugal rights. Tarben's self-control in the face of his obvious desire was an impressive display of restraint — as was his patience. Ronan kept expecting the man to unleash his anger at every slight, large or small, that Ronan delivered more boldly each time. Yet Tarben hadn't raised his hand, even in warning. It left Ronan wondering perversely where the line might be where Tarben would lose his temper.

"Move out!" Tarben pressed his arm against Ronan's mid-section as he kicked his horse into a slow walk.

As they rode through the abbey's gates, the Dark Mountains warriors fanned out in what Ronan recognized as a diamond formation and sped into a trot. His tutors had given up teaching him warfare tactics when he'd shown no interest or aptitude. He did remember that this was a classic way to move a small group of people where one or more in particular needed to be protected. With him and Tarben situated in the middle, anyone trying to attack would have to go through some number of soldiers before reaching them. Ronan was both safeguarded and trapped. Even if he could manage to slip Tarben's hold, he would never make it past his men, regardless of the direction he ran. *It's okay. I don't have to rescue myself. Uncle Soren will come for me.* He was certain that his father wouldn't simply give in to the demands of the Dark Mountains king. One way or another, Ronan was going to be liberated. He only had to stay alive.

"We have a hard day's ride today. It will be relatively slow but relentless until night starts to fall. Tomorrow will be much the same. We need to reach my father's castle as quickly as possible."

"Of course. The sooner we arrive, the sooner your father can send mine the ransom demand."

"The offer of a treaty."

"Semantics." Ronan looked over his shoulder. "That means —"

"I know what it means." It was the first time Ronan had heard anything close to testiness in the man's tone.

He turned to look forward again. "My apologies. I didn't intend to be condescending."

"I know what that word means, too, and I took no offense." The man's tone implied otherwise.

Ronan couldn't help smiling. This was the first hint of the Dark Mountains man lacking any amount of confidence. His glee died quickly, however. It wasn't in him to be petty, and he'd been taught to be gracious in all matters when dealing with those who lacked what he'd been blessed with. "I've had a lot of classroom learning so that I can help my brother when it's his time to rule. I'm not good at warfare, so a ministry position it is." As soon as he'd finished with his explanation, sadness stole over him. All of this meant nothing if he was forced to remain in the Dark Mountains.

"You aren't built to be a warrior."

That point was evident as he sat in front of the man, dwarfed by his size. Although he'd gained some height in recent years, Ronan wasn't as tall as his brother or other male family members. And he remained slender, regardless of how much he ate or how active he was. Maybe this was a plan set by the gods all along, to make him ready to fulfill this unexpected role as wife to a foreign warrior. The idea fit, especially given his desire to lie only with men, and not just that, but with a man in particular who could protect and pamper him.

No. Ronan inwardly shook his head. That made no sense. His nature couldn't be something destined to be less worthy. His cousin Nora was far more athletic than he, and her fate was both one of wife and a position that wielded great power. Surely the gods didn't equate physical and emotional softness with sex. He was different, that's all, and if he'd been born first, Morlen would be sitting on top of this horse, not he — although his brother would probably be trussed like a dressed deer and slung over the saddle to be kept under control. Ronan had made this whole affair easy for his captor.

A thought occurred to him, making his skin go cold. "What are you going to do with me once we reach your king's seat of power?"

"I don't understand the question."

Ronan licked his lips, trying to decide if it made sense to ask a more pointed one and perhaps give Tarben bad ideas. He decided to tackle the issue head on. "Are you going to lock me in the dungeon?"

Tarben pressed his arm more tightly against him. "Why would I put my wife in the dungeon?" He seemed genuinely perplexed at the idea.

"To keep me from running away." His husband might not be as bright as he seemed, even with his good vocabulary.

"You can't do that. You *will not* do that. Our mountain home is treacherous ground, with many hidden cliffs and dangerous animals. Even if you were to memorize the path we take on the journey there, you could easily get lost."

Ronan huffed. "I may not be good at fighting, but I do have an excellent sense of direction."

By way of response, Tarben shifted his arm so that his hand rested against Ronan's chin. The skin-to-skin touch caused a wave of excitement that shamed Ronan, even as it delighted him. "Look up. See that mist rising with the dawn?"

He did see it. There was a haunting beauty to the way the morning dew swirled around the treetops. "Yes," was all he said, closing his eyes briefly to bask in Tarben's touch — a guilty moment of pleasure that he quashed on his next breath.

"Those of us raised here know every inch of these mountains. We explore them as part of our warrior training through many seasons. We can find our way blindfolded, quite literally. If attacked, we can lose ourselves in the mist and even lead our pursuers to their doom." Tarben tightened his hold briefly before dropping his arm again. "However I have manhandled you, I want you to understand that I don't want you to die. And you will be treated with all the courtesy that your station demands."

Ronan believed him. He shouldn't, yet he did. Tarben had coddled him more than was necessary for his intended goals. It wasn't only the fact that he hadn't forced himself upon Ronan. There were subtler ways that he hadn't missed. He'd had an opportunity to bathe that morning, being escorted by the same cheery nun to a small chamber where a steaming tub of water waited for him. It was lovely to wash the grime of his journey off, as well as wash and braid his hair. And the nun had brought him clean clothes, hemmed by her at Tarben's request to fit Ronan's smaller body. He wasn't entirely sure where the shirt and trousers had come from, but the fact that Tarben had thought to pamper him in this small way was surprising and disarming. *Maybe he was tired of me smelling.* The fact that Tarben's men held the kind of musky male odor that came from riding for days on end and wearing the same clothing made that possibility unlikely, although the man himself had obviously washed before coming to bed the previous night. *Was that for my benefit?*

"It doesn't matter," he finally responded. "I'm a prisoner either way."

"I would like to think that the difference between a soft, warm bed and a cold, hard pallet has *some* meaning."

"That depends. Are you in the bed, too? Because if you are, I might prefer the dungeon." He regretted his words the moment they came out of his mouth, then immediately became annoyed at himself. There was no reason for him to regret anything he said or did to Tarben. He was the aggrieved party and had no obligation to take care with Tarben's sensibilities.

Tarben leaned over to speak directly into Ronan's ear, his warm breath tickling his skin and sending a shiver down his spine. "I will sleep next to you, wife, no matter where you bed down."

"Huh!" Ronan tried to show distain for that promise, even as heat caused his cock to stir. Fortunately, the man said nothing more on the subject, and Ronan was wise enough not to bait him any further. He didn't seem to be able to come out on top for any topic they sparred over.

Almost as one, Tarben and his men slowed their horses back to a walk. "We need to pace our mounts."

"You needn't explain that to me. I do understand the basics of warfare. It's not like I have any say in what you do, either."

"That is not entirely true, wife. When traveling with a…someone other than a warrior, we are solicitous of them. If you need to relieve yourself, tell me. We will stop briefly for that. I don't want you to be uncomfortable—any more than you already are," he added, almost under his breath.

"You will be the first to know of my bodily needs," Ronan replied as coolly as he could. It was getting harder and harder to remain aloof, something that he dared not become complacent about. He was literally in the arms of his enemy. He must not lose sight of that.

* * * *

"The melt water causes even a small river like this to be dangerous." Tarben issued the warning while placing a clean cloth and soap on the grassy bank.

44

Beside them, he added a rolled-up night rail. "This is for you. I'll have one of my men wash the tunic you have on so that you have it clean for tomorrow."

Ronan stared at the items. "I don't wear women's clothing." He folded his arms and glared at him. This was how the whole day had gone. The boy ran hot and cold when it came to their interactions, not that anyone could blame him.

Tarben strived for patience. "I understand, but the abbey had little in the way of men's attire. This night rail is plain and thick. The nuns don't pamper themselves with frilly garments, so it's not as if it will make you look like a woman overly much. And more importantly, it will help keep you warm through the night."

"I thought that was your job."

All Mother save me! Did his wife even know how coquettish he was being with statements like that? Tarben's hard dick pulsed with an aching need that hadn't abated all day. "Is that an invitation for me to drape your body like a blanket?" He knew some satisfaction as Ronan's cheeks reddened and he looked away. That feeling was quickly overcome by guilt, something that plagued him constantly. *It can't be helped.*

He waited until Ronan had stripped down to his skin before doing the same. His men had strict orders to remain watchful for danger without peeking at his wife. It might seem ludicrous for him to impose such prudish limitations, given that they were all men, yet Tarben couldn't shake the feeling that he needed to treat Ronan as he would a woman. It was a matter of husbandly duty to protect his wife's modesty and life alike. And being a prince, Ronan was surely used to a great deal of consideration, if not outright pampering.

Allowing him privacy while he washed away the dust of their day's journey in icy waters seemed little enough.

It was hard not to stare as the boy waded into the rushing water with soap in hand. This was the first chance Tarben had to see the whole of him, and the sight made his tongue stick to the roof of his mouth and his hard dick to somehow become even more so. Sleeping next to his wife the night before without touching him had been difficult. Now that he knew for a certainty what he was missing, it would be torturous. Still, he would keep himself under control. He'd already crossed many lines of honorable behavior. He wouldn't add rape to the litany of shameful acts. That was something that his father and his duty to his people could not force him to do. If the Moorcondians didn't recognize their marriage for lack of consummation — a concept neither he nor his father had known of — then so be it. As long as they managed to gain even a short-term treaty, it would be enough. He could return Ronan to his home a free man, with this nightmare behind them both.

There was a throb in both his dick and his heart at the thought of letting the prince go. He recognized the reaction as possessiveness. It made him want to go and grab the boy, hold him close and bed him right there on the grassy banks. The urge scared him. He wasn't one to let his emotions or desires get in the way of duty and honor. A cooling off was needed, so he strode into the freezing water without hesitation and plunged through the curtain of melt water cascading over an outcrop of rocks. The cold robbed him of his breath, but it also made his cock shrivel and sent his balls to seek warmth up between his legs. He stood there heaving harsh breaths as he waited to make sure his body was completely subdued. He could just make out Ronan's shadow beyond the waterfall as the boy splashed water on himself.

Although his blood was turning to ice while he stood, Tarben wouldn't give in to the desire to return to land and the relative warmth of the evening air. He was determined to stay there until his cock and balls fell off, if necessary. It was imperative that he get himself under control. Not only did he not want to alarm his wife with his hard-on, but it was embarrassing, too. As a jarl, he'd always been careful in how, where and when he slaked his needs. It was hard to know if a bed partner was there because they wanted to be or if it was merely to appease a powerful man. He was used to going long periods where he relied on his hand for pleasure. That wasn't a possible solution under the circumstances, so his choice was to make it clear to all that he wanted his wife with unrelenting need or to pretend he was unaffected. Pride alone dictated the latter solution.

Over the sound of rushing water, he detected another sound. Having spent the better part of his life living outdoors, all his senses were attuned to nature. Survival depended on it. Tarben raced out of the waterfall before his brain even registered what was happening. He was driven by the urgency to reach Ronan, and he swept the startled boy off his feet and over to the bank as a rock from above came crashing down. They both stared at it as it landed right where Ronan had been only a moment before, spraying water all around the area with the force of it. Tarben wrapped a shivering Ronan tightly within his embrace as they both caught their breath. He scanned the area above the waterfall, looking for an explanation as to why the rock had fallen. A flash of something caught his eye, then vanished with his next blink. Try as he might, there was nothing to see except startled birds.

Ronan leaned into him, resting his head on Tarben's shoulder. "What...how...?"

Tarben rubbed his hand down the boy's back in what he hoped was a soothing gesture. "The water is swift. Give it sufficient time and it can carve through rock and loosen even the biggest of boulders." He looked around them some more, alert to any danger.

There was nothing out of the ordinary to see, however. There was really no reason to continue to hold the prince in his arms, yet he was loath to let him go. He convinced himself it was to warm the boy, but really it was more selfish than that. Ronan's skin was soft to touch, not like the roughness of other men, even those who were willing to be mounted by Tarben. It reminded him of how he remembered his mother and sister felt while he was still young enough to hug them close. And Ronan smelled nice, as well, some kind of flowery scent. It was his hair, Tarben realized. The nuns had given him soap that had been far nicer and more fragrant than what Tarben had pulled out of his saddlebag. As a warrior, all he needed was something to remove the worst of the stink and dirt.

Because he could feel the effects of his frigid bathing starting to erode, he reluctantly set Ronan away from him, although keeping a hold on one arm, and led him over to where their clothing lay. He grabbed the drying cloth and wrapped it around Ronan's slender shoulders. Then, instead of doing the smart thing and leaving his wife to do the rest, he began rubbing him dry. He would have expected the boy to bat his efforts away as he'd done earlier when Tarben had tried to help him. The fact that Ronan remained passive worried him.

"Are you all right? Did I hurt you?" Tarben kept his eye on his task and not on Ronan's expression. He tried to ensure that his efforts remained as impersonal as possible so as not to upset the boy — and for himself. He didn't really want to see any hatred his wife might feel for him at the moment. The passiveness might merely be from shock and not appreciation for his efforts.

"It landed right where I was standing. I didn't hear a thing. If you hadn't grabbed me, I would have been killed." Ronan's voice had a faraway quality.

Tarben glanced up as he knelt to dry Ronan's legs, trying not to look at the slender shaft lying limp near his face. "Perhaps." He moved down to the calves. "I'm used to the sounds of this forest, so I moved quickly when I heard something that wasn't right." He froze when Ronan's hand landed on his shoulder.

"Thank you. I know that you have to keep me safe if your scheme is to work…"

Tarben stood abruptly, hating that his sudden movement startled Ronan. "I would not have you harmed, no matter the situation." He sighed and looked away. "I know it doesn't matter to you, and it shouldn't, given the circumstances, but I am truly sorry for all of this."

Ronan didn't respond immediately. For a while they stood silently, the only sounds those of nature around them. "I believe you." Ronan reached to tug the drying cloth from Tarben's hands. "I'll finish with this. You must be cold as well. And I'll wear the night rail. You're right that it will be warm, and if I can wear a clean tunic tomorrow, it will make the journey a little more pleasant."

Tarben had to force his fingers to uncurl, such was his intense desire to hold on to the cloth and finish the task himself. Sense won out, and he left his wife to dry off and dress. He did the same, except he kept his eyes and ears on alert, making sure nothing suspicious was happening. There was no reason to doubt that the falling rock was anything other than a natural occurrence, and yet... The old warriors talked about having an instinct for danger. He'd come to believe that they weren't simply telling tales. With something as important as Ronan's safety, he couldn't be too cautious.

When they were dressed, he escorted his wife back to camp. His men were already roasting strips of fresh game and baking root vegetables among the firewood. Someone had laid out his bedroll with an extra fur placed upon it. He gave an approving nod inside his head. At least his core group of warriors understood that Ronan was to be treated with the same care that they would extend to a woman traveling with them — not that the Moorcondian prince was female, their marriage notwithstanding. And Tarben could see strength in the boy. He'd shown remarkable poise under the circumstances, and that was worthy of respect, no matter what. Still, Tarben couldn't shake the feeling that Ronan needed and deserved to be cared for. And as a man of the Dark Mountains, Tarben had been raised with expectations of how a man saw to his wife's needs and protection. Ronan's sex wasn't going to erase that ingrained sense of duty and honor.

Tarben guided Ronan to sit on the pallet and made sure the boy's cloak was wrapped securely around him. Because his wife hadn't washed his hair in the river, there was nothing to cause him extra chill, unlike Tarben himself, who longed to dry out completely by the fire. "Wait here. Please," he added, because courtesy cost him nothing. "I'll bring you your evening meal once it's done. In the meantime, I have something to do."

Ronan didn't look at him as he said, "You don't need to explain yourself to me. And obviously, I'm not going anywhere," he added with a sweep of his arm that encompassed the warriors ranged around the camp.

Tarben grimaced at the return of their chilly relationship that had nothing to do with the weather. Instead of uselessly trying to explain that as his wife, Ronan had the right to explanations and that Tarben was duty-bound to answer to the boy in some ways, he kept silent. It would be pointless, given the circumstances. There was no way that Ronan would view himself as anything other than Tarben's captive. So he left to find Alf and pulled him aside to speak privately.

"Look after the jarlina. I need to explore something."

Great warrior that he was, his right-hand man was blunt. "What is the danger? Surely the Moorcondians couldn't have figured out where the prince is already."

Tarben scanned the area, scrutinizing the men under his command. "No, that's not what I'm worried about. There is no reason for the Moorcondians to think we have the prince until we send word to them of it. They'll be looking for someone more local, I'll wager, before they wonder if it's a foreign act." He looked at Alf once more. "And it's my wife's safety that concerns me, not ours." He quickly relayed what had happened at the river.

"My lord, I don't have to remind you that this time of year, the melt water causes all kinds of instability in the rivers that it feeds into."

"I know." Tarben tried not to let his irritation show. "It's not my head at work on this. It's here." He patted his gut. "I need to take a look."

"I understand, jarl. Have no concern. I will guard the jarlina with my life."

Tarben thumped him on the back. "You're a good man, Alf. I trust no one else to do so."

With that, he returned quickly to the river, climbing up to the top of the cliff where the waterfall cascaded. It was treacherous going, even the vegetated land around it being prone to loose detritus that he only navigated successfully because of his life-long training doing so. As he went, he looked for signs that someone had come before him and did the same when he reached the top. He was a good tracker, but not the best. And while he saw no signs of anything amiss, he also knew that those truly skilled in tracking others through the dense forest were excellent at hiding their own recent presence.

Tarben spent more time looking before the fading light made it both futile and risky to continue to do so. When he returned to camp, he found his wife much as he'd left him, Alf standing nearby with arms folded and a clear warning to others etched across his face. He remained where he was, even though Tarben had returned, because Ronan hadn't yet been served supper. The others milled around, waiting as was proper, for Tarben to serve his wife first. *My wife.* It was weird to think of the prince in those terms, and yet also somehow very, very right in Tarben's mind. He took care, as he'd been taught to do, to pick the most tender pieces of meat and vegetables for Ronan and plate them on a piece of cleaned bark. They were living rough, but there was always a way to accommodate more refined tastes and needs.

He squatted in front of Ronan and held out his offering. "Here is your meal. It's not much…"

Ronan snatched it from him and put a piece of meat in his mouth, chewed and swallowed. "Thank you," he said, before taking more. It was a bit grudging, and there was no eye contact, let alone a friendly expression. But his enthusiastic consumption of the food was all that mattered to Tarben. As he watched his wife eat, he felt a new sense of pride. Providing for a wife and children was the core measure of a man's life. It came even above loyalty to one's king. Tarben had long ago found peace with the knowledge that he would never be a father. And he'd assumed that if he ever did forge a life-long commitment with another man, it would be with a warrior — or at least a man who was capable of fending for himself. He might be selling Ronan short, but there was something vulnerable in the boy. It brought out all Tarben's instincts to protect. Far from dismissing them, he found he wanted to embrace them. However their union had come about, he was determined to be a good husband to Ronan.

Chapter Four

Ronan had awoken feeling surprisingly well-rested. It hadn't been a long sleep, Tarben and his men breaking camp just as the sun was rising, yet Ronan had slept deeply and warmly pressed against Tarben's body. As with the previous night, there had been no overtures on Tarben's part, although his hard dick had poked at the small of Ronan's back, a constant reminder that the man wanted him. Ronan had fallen asleep while lying stiffly beside his captor, expecting him to take some liberties, even with his men all around them. It seemed impossible that such an overtly masculine man wouldn't seek to find pleasure with someone bound to him physically and, at least in this country, legally. That Tarben hadn't done so was both a relief and disturbingly disappointing. It didn't help that he was again also aroused when woken. He was sure Tarben knew that inconvenient fact, too, except that unlike the previous morning when they'd been alone, the man ignored it.

Ronan sat cross-legged on the bedroll, eating a simple meal of oatcakes, berries and some of the meat that had been dried overnight. All around him, the Dark Mountains warriors efficiently prepared to leave. They were a remarkably disciplined group, talking little and focused on their tasks. They ignored Ronan, which was how it had been the night before when Tarben had left the camp to do the gods knew what. Ronan had known a moment of almost panic as he'd watched Tarben disappearing into the woods. For the first time, he'd been alone with these rough, foreign men. He had braced for at least leers and perhaps baiting words, yet none had come. The only sign that any of them remembered he existed had been the silent presence of Tarben's obviously right-hand man, standing behind Ronan like a mini mountain until Tarben had returned. At the time, Ronan had assumed that the man was there to keep him from leaving. Upon reflection, it felt as if he had been there to protect him, although from whom or what was hard to say.

Ronan shivered a bit at the memory of how close he'd come to being killed by the boulder. The near accident had been shocking. Never in his life had he come so close to being seriously hurt. Even during his relatively brief training as a soldier, he'd always felt safe. His Uncle Soren had made a point of involving himself, carefully orchestrating the lessons to ensure Ronan's safety. It had been embarrassing at the time, because he was certain the same thing hadn't been done for Morlen. Everyone seemed to know that he had no aptitude for fighting. And still, it had been a relief when his father had summoned him and declared that such lessons had come to an end. Trying to keep up with his brother's skill and everyone else's expectations had been exhausting.

So no, Ronan was not cut out for being a soldier and had never experienced anything remotely life-threatening. And as disturbing as seeing the large rock hit the spot in the water where he'd been a moment before had been, being held by Tarben had been somehow worse. Their wet bodies had slipped against one another, sending sparks of something other than fear coursing through him. That reaction had scared him more than nearly being crushed to death. He should hate Tarben. The man had stolen first his body, then his voice during the sham wedding ceremony. That sort of contemptible conduct was worthy of never-ending opprobrium. Ronan should despise Tarben and fight him at every turn. Instead, he'd stood clinging to the man, comforted by his embrace and struggling against arousal that had threatened to erupt, despite the fear and the cold. And when the warrior had rubbed him dry, Ronan had had to resist being lulled into contentment. If the gods intended to punish him for his weaknesses, they had found the perfect way.

A large hand came into his line of vision. "Come. We must leave if you are finished breaking your fast."

Ronan looked up at Tarben before popping the last of his oatcake into his mouth. He wanted to ignore the offer of help, but instead reached for that hand and allowed his captor to haul him to his feet. "Thank you." He gave himself another moment to enjoy the contact before tugging free. He followed Tarben to his horse. "Another long day, I presume?"

"Yes. It gets harder from here as we head up the side of the mountain." Tarben no longer tried to help Ronan into the saddle. A quick study, apparently, and yet Ronan perversely missed the effort.

When the man hauled himself up behind him and wrapped his arm around Ronan's waist, he didn't try to sit away from him. He now knew that eventually he would end up leaning against him, so it would be a waste of energy. Instead, Ronan settled against Tarben's chest and got as comfortable as he could. He smiled briefly at a low grumble that sounded as if his so-called husband was discomforted. *Good.* As petty as it was, Ronan figured that if he couldn't be happy, they may as well both be miserable. Once a warrior tied the bedroll to Tarben's saddle, they got under way.

This time, there was no trotting. The road, such as it was, narrowed too much to permit them all to stick to it. That meant that most of Tarben's men rode through the trees, the snippets of sunlight dappling through the canopy gleaming off their helmets. The morning mist hadn't entirely burned off yet, either, which obscured the men even more. There was something otherworldly about it all, yet cradled as he was in Tarben's arms, he still felt safe. It was a perturbing situation. Being a captive should have given him an unrelenting fear for his life. So why didn't it? Surely it was folly to think that Tarben would take care of him. Ronan's abduction was a means to an end that hadn't been crafted for his benefit. All of which begged the question of; if there were a treaty, what then?

"How is this all supposed to end?" He asked the question by turning his head enough to direct it toward Tarben.

"With a treaty," was the gruff reply.

Ronan strived for patience. "Yes, yes, I understand that's your goal for your country. What about me?"

He'd almost said 'us', but that would have been dumb. They were not together, not in any way that he recognized.

"You are my wife."

"Not as far as I'm concerned." Ronan didn't even try to keep the bitterness out of his voice. "Is your intent to keep me hostage for the rest of my life?" The idea that he might never see his family other than through brief and orchestrated visits, or live in his country again, caused his heart to skip a beat.

There was some hesitation before the answer, as if Tarben hadn't thought that far ahead. "Not a hostage, no."

Ronan huffed out his frustration. "But if my father gives you the terms you want and promises to honor them even if I am returned but you refuse to give me back, then how am I not still a captive? My life would be forfeit if my country breaks the terms. That is the fate of treaty brides."

Tarben's hold on him briefly tightened. "No harm will come to you. You have my word on that."

"But I want to go home." Ronan hated the nearly pleading tone of his voice.

Again, Tarben's arm squeezed him. "You are my wife." As answers went, it was hardly illuminating or reassuring. The man should have easily been able to say that he'd return Ronan to Moorcondia and good riddance. It couldn't be that the man wanted Ronan if his country could have its treaty without keeping him a hostage.

"You can't want me forever. Surely you look forward to having a wife who can give you children."

"I care not about becoming a father. I spend more time patrolling our boarders than in my father's castle, and I see how hard that life is on other men and their families. Besides, the young warriors I train are like sons. It gives me the experience of raising them without the fear that I'll drop them on their tiny heads."

Ronan couldn't help smiling at that statement. "However you may style yourself, you are a prince, like me. Are you not expected to add members to the royal family?" Ronan certainly was. The idea of wedding a woman and giving her children was one of the aspects of his life that he dreaded most. He had no real understanding of what to do with a woman in bed, no matter the bawdy tales of other men, and had no wish to experience it.

"My brother is my father's heir and has two daughters so far. He and his wife are likely to produce at least one son eventually. If not, our sister has three of her own among the five in her brood. The oldest of those would take the throne. Our line is already secure."

"What about your nieces? Aren't they permitted to rule the Dark Mountains?"

"No. Women are spiritual leaders, healers and advisors. But they cannot be queens in their own right."

Ronan made a point of turning his head so that his frown could show. "That hardly seems fair."

Tarben glanced down at him, his eyes one of the few features visible given his helmet and nose plate. "When the fate of a country relies on its king's sword arm, it's fair."

"Oh." Ronan face forward again. "I suppose so, although there are women soldiers in my father's army. I wouldn't want to go against one of them — and neither should you."

Tarben nudged Ronan's head with his chin. "Look to the far left. See that warrior in front? That is a woman."

"Really?" Ronan craned his neck to get a better look at her. She was indistinguishable from the others. "I wouldn't have guessed."

"Exactly. She is as big as a man and as strong as most of my warriors. How many women do you think are like she is, both capable of being a warrior and wishing to do so? They are few and far between. Add that unlikelihood to the royal line and you can understand why we have only been ruled by men."

"Hmm. Well, it could happen at some point, then what would your people do?"

"I have no idea and will be long dead anyway. Others will decide, and I am fine with that. I have no aptitude for ruling, only fighting."

You're certainly built for it. Ronan would have cut off his own tongue before admitting that out loud. It was too much of a compliment, and he needed to remember that they were enemies. And they had veered off topic. "Forget children, then. Do you not want a woman in your bed? Surely sleeping next to me is a duty and nothing more."

"Duty, yes. It's the 'nothing more' that you misunderstand."

Ronan felt his cheeks heating. "Men's cocks are mindless beasts. They get hard at the least provocation. And I know that soldiers make do with each other when away campaigning. That doesn't mean they don't want a woman waiting for them when they come home."

"That is true, but I am the kind of man who has no interest in women. I enjoy their company, of course, but

I don't want to find one in my bed." The infuriating man leaned down to whisper in Ronan's ear. "Your ass is far more enticing."

Ronan squeaked in outrage, earning him quick looks from those around them. He had to drop his gaze to hide his discomfort. "How vulgar."

"But true." Tarben seemed almost pleased with the reaction he'd achieved.

Ronan stayed quiet for a while, silently steaming, yet also aware of his own reaction to Tarben's declaration. Thank the gods his smallclothes kept his dick from rising up to poke at Tarben's arm. Finally, he felt under control enough to ask the most obvious question. "So are you saying you intend to keep me for the rest of my life?" He held his breath as he waited for an answer, although he wasn't even sure what kind he was hoping for.

The man's response confirmed Ronan's earlier thought. "I am saying that I have not thought that far ahead."

Disappointed, yet tired of the strain their talk was causing, Ronan held his tongue and let the steady gait of the horse lull him.

* * * *

Tarben brought his cadre to a halt in the late afternoon where their path home diverged into two. He stared at them both, contemplating which to take. When he'd started on this unenviable journey, he'd led his warriors to Moorcondia via the fastest route, with the intention to do the same on the way back. Time was not on their side, but the quickest passage was also the more dangerous one. It was steep and, while relatively easily navigated for their sure-footed horses and seasoned warriors, he couldn't quite let go of what had happened the night before at the river. Even though he'd detected nothing amiss, his instincts continued to warn him that his wife's safety was at risk. The boy, who had every reason to hate and fear him, lounged against his chest in boneless fashion. No matter what his biting tongue said, Ronan's body displayed a level of trust that enhanced Tarben's natural inclination to be a protector.

Adding another day's ride would make little difference. "We go left, around the mountain." He issued the order in a curt voice, knowing that his warriors wouldn't hesitate to obey, even as they would wonder about his decision. And they did, all of them steering their mounts without hesitation in the direction he'd ordered and continuing their journey at the same slow, constant pace.

As the sun began to set, they came upon the outskirts of a village that he'd forgotten even existed. He hadn't passed this way in many years. None of them had, he'd wager. Few warriors came from such a small farming community, but the villagers recognized them immediately. Each person they passed stopped what they were doing to bring an end to their day, silently respectful and bowing their heads when they caught sight of him. If they were curious about the foreign and richly cloaked boy sitting practically on his lap, they didn't show it. No one said anything, and while their reticence could be explained by their awe of a jarl and his warriors, Tarben could see in their faces how tired and weak they were. There was no point in expending more energy than was necessary under these conditions.

He brought his warriors to a halt when he spied what had to be the headman standing outside the main building with head bowed, holding the arm of an old woman. Tarben knew she was the matriarch of the village, the oldest living woman. Her tiny, frail form swam in her clothing. It was astounding that she'd survived the winter. Yet her eyes were bright and her expression proud as she gazed directly at him. Tarben showed her the respect she was due by inclining his head when he stopped.

"Good wife, master headman, please excuse our sudden incursion. We are returning to the king's castle and take this path as the safest one for our honored…" He almost said 'guest' but that wasn't right. "For my wife." The word still sat strangely on his tongue.

The headman wasn't able to hide his surprise, although he quickly banked it. The old woman gave him an assessing look before doing the same to Ronan, who sat straighter under the scrutiny, yet said nothing. "We are honored, Jarl Tarben," the headman said with another bow of his head.

More people crowded in next to them, openly curious now. Their gaunt faces and sunken eyes were hard to see, but at least his presence was proving to be a distraction for them. *Not me. Ronan is the curiosity.* "My warriors and I will be making camp just beyond your far border. We will not impose on you." It was critical to make that clear, because he could see the calculation in the headman's eyes as to how many more mouths would need feeding.

Raising his hand, Tarben beckoned the man at his back. Alf rode to his side immediately and leaned over for instructions. "Give them all that we have," Tarben said in a low voice.

Alf nodded once before issuing the orders to the others. If he thought Tarben's largesse was overreaching, he knew better than to say anything. All his warriors did, although he detected some resentment from those who were not part of his core group as they unpacked their saddlebags and laid food at the feet of the old woman. There were murmurs from the crowd around them—excited ones—and a few people even managed to smile at the growing pile.

"Please accept what little we have." Tarben directed his words toward the woman, knowing that she was the one who controlled the dispensing of food resources.

The woman's expression didn't change, but her response spoke volumes. "You have a strong sense of duty, jarl. It is known." With that, she hobbled back to the hut behind her, two women taking over her care.

The headman once more bowed, this time lower than was necessary. "We are most grateful, jarl."

Hating that his people were in such desperate straits that a meager offering was like a feast, Tarben said nothing more. He simply nodded once again and kicked his horse into motion. His men hurried to do the same now that they'd given all their food. It wasn't until they had cleared the village proper that Ronan spoke up.

"Those people are starving, aren't they?" His voice was soft, yet filled with emotion.

"Yes," Tarben replied simply because what more was there to say?

"It's time to tell me everything." Ronan swiveled his head to glare at him. "I deserve to know." His tone made it clear that he wasn't going to let the matter go, nor should he.

"When we make camp, I will tell you."

Turning around again, Ronan said, "Yes, you will." Then he leaned against Tarben once more, a strange show of trust that Tarben appreciated. It was the one bright spot in an otherwise miserable situation.

* * * *

Ronan glanced at the food Tarben offered him on a piece of bark, then stared into Tarben's eyes. The prince's directness was surprisingly unnerving. There was something about his eyes... Tarben nearly dropped the make-shift plate. His sudden clumsiness surprised and irked him. His men were watching everything, even as they pretended to be focused on their own meals. It wouldn't do for them to see how much his wife affected him.

"That's too much for me."

The ridiculous statement brought Tarben's concentration back into focus. "Nonsense. You will eat it all." He shoved the piece of bark in Ronan's face.

Surprisingly, his wife actually took it, then placed it on his cross-legged lap. "Unless you're prepared to shove it down my throat, I'll eat what I want, and you should have the rest." He kept his voice low, intimate even, for Tarben's ears only. "Why don't you sit down now so that we can share it?"

Tarben blinked rapidly to clear his vision, because he could swear there was a coquettish look on his wife's face. *Impossible.* The boy hated him, but he understood duty, too, no doubt. And as it was a sensible offer, Tarben did as asked, folding his legs under him to sit opposite Ronan. The Moorcondian prince set the piece of bark on the ground between them before picking up a piece of meat and taking a bite. Tarben was momentarily transfixed by the movement of his wife's lips and the flick of his tongue to lap at some juices that dibbled down.

"You aren't eating."

Tarben automatically bristled at the censure and command in the tone until he reminded himself that he'd married a prince of a powerful country, not some lower noble. However placid the boy might appear, he'd proven to be anything but. And of course, he was used to being obeyed by nearly everyone. So Tarben let it go and began to pick at the food. As hungry as he was, there was no way he was going to take food from his wife's mouth until he was certain that he'd had his fill first.

Ronan ate in silence for a while before finally broaching the topic of what had happened in the village. "Tell me what's going on." He lifted his gaze. "Please. I deserve to know the truth of why your country needs that treaty so badly that you resorted to...*this*."

Tarben swallowed both his mouthful of food and a sigh. If he let himself think about it too much, he'd have to face the fact that he was mentally exhausted over the entire mess. "Two growing seasons ago, virtually every crop we had was decimated by some fungal blight. Nothing that we tried helped to save them, and the harvest was meager. Our stores of food got us through the winter, and we hoped, of course, that it had been eradicated by the affected plants being burned. And that was true, but the next season was unusually wet. Our soil eroded more than usual, and the crops once more failed in large numbers." He glanced up at the night sky, seeing that storm clouds were coming. "This season has proven to be little better."

Ronan cocked his head. "So, that's what you want from a treaty, food?"

"Yes. We have little to trade, except timber and stone, but we thought it would get us enough food to keep our people from starving as we regain our agriculture." Tarben concentrated on his meal so that his wife couldn't see the fury in his eyes that he felt whenever he thought of how his father's overtures had been rejected.

"But…Moorcondia has always come to its neighbors' aid when asked. A treaty that gave us building materials would be welcome."

Tarben lifted his gaze. "And yet, your father turned away our envoy several times. The last one was killed for his efforts."

Ronan's breath hitched. "He would never do such a thing!"

Tarben merely shrugged. He didn't have the energy to get into a fight with his wife. The facts were what they were. And as diplomacy wasn't his domain, he didn't bother to defend what he'd been told. "It doesn't matter what happened. The survival of our people is at stake." He swept his hand to indicate the warriors around them. "We can live for as long as necessary off what nature has. Those villagers cannot. There are too many mouths and not enough time to hunt and gather to feed them all. There was a time when our ancestors didn't farm. Those days are long over. If we can't sustain ourselves until our crop yield returns, we die.

"I won't let that happen," he added, leaning toward Ronan so that the boy could understand how resolute he was on the matter.

To his credit, Ronan didn't shy away. In fact, he likewise brought his face closer to him. "I won't let it happen, either. If you had taken the time to explain this to me instead of rendering me unconscious and forcing me into marriage, I would have agreed to help on principle."

Taken aback by the obviously earnestness of the Moorcondian's declaration, Tarben could only stare mutely for a long while. Staring into his wife's lovely green eyes, he once more got lost in them — and his dick hardened. That was nothing new. The fact that he'd been soft during the conversation up until this moment was the surprising part. He believed Ronan, but it didn't matter what a second prince wanted. King Auden would do as he pleased, and he'd shown that he at best was indifferent to the Dark Mountains' suffering. He couldn't let the man's fetching son disabuse him of that fact. What he did for his people remained necessary.

Tarben forced himself to sit back. "That may be so, but you lack the power to bind a treaty between our people. This is the only way forward."

"You underestimate me," Ronan huffed.

"Never. It's simply a matter of the hard truth. And you are not alone in your lack of control. It's not my place to change the path laid before me by my father, either."

Ronan huffed out a breath. "I'll prove you both wrong, then."

"I sincerely hope so." He meant the words. The more time he spent in Ronan's company, the less he liked what he'd been forced into doing. At the time his father had called him to his council room, his orders had seemed unreal, like a dream. He'd started his journey not truly understanding what he was about to do, nor appreciating how much of his honor he was going to sacrifice. He vowed to himself at that moment to do whatever he could to achieve his country's goals without sacrificing Ronan's freedom any more than he already had. And yet, the thought of letting the boy go caused his heart to squeeze painfully. He had to force himself to eat and turn off that part of him in both his head and his loins that wanted to scream 'no'.

Chapter Five

"Is it going to rain like this all day?" Ronan hated how pathetic he sounded, but he wasn't used to waking up on wet ground with water dripping in his face.

Tarben ate a handful of berries before answering. Because they'd given all their oatcakes and dried meat to the villagers, they had little in the way of food, other than what had been freshly killed the night before and foraged that morning. "No, it won't." Before Ronan could feel relief, the infuriating man added, "It will be pouring before the sun finishes rising."

"Wonderful." Ronan was too tired and miserable to pretend that the news didn't bother him. As there was nothing to be done about it, he finished his own meager meal before reaching for his boots. He'd tugged one on, then grabbed the other. Before he could bring it to his foot, Tarben kicked it out of his hand. Ronan first gasped, then glared, and his heart stopped when Tarben pulled his knife out of his belt and threw it down. Following its trajectory with his mouth agape,

Ronan saw the blade pierce the skull of a snake that was slithering out of his boot.

"Gods, what is that?"

Tarben didn't answer right away. He stood with arms akimbo, his chest heaving. "A tree snake. They are deadly poisonous."

"Oh." The danger he'd been in dawned on him with force enough to cause him to nearly whimper. He had to press his hand to his mouth to keep the noise in.

"Are you hurt?" Grabbing him by the shoulders, Tarben hauled him to his feet. "Did it bite you?" He ran his hands down Ronan's arms to scrutinize his fingers and palms.

"N-no." Ronan shook his head. "I didn't see or feel anything before you kicked it away. You saved my life?" It didn't seem possible that he'd come so close to death...and from such a simple thing as a snake bite.

Tarben eased his grip and blew out a breath as he stood back. "I saw the movement out of the corner of my eye. It was a near thing," he added in a thick voice. The man seemed nearly as shaken as Ronan.

Alf approached, Ronan's boot in one hand and the headless snake in another. "It will make for good eating this evening."

Ronan made a face. "You eat them?"

"Not normally, Jarlina. They are hard to find, living in trees as they do. They're shy and not typically aggressive unless disturbed in their nests." The warrior frowned as he looked around the open area where they'd made camp. "They rarely venture this far out of the forest."

"No," Tarben agreed, "they don't. It's not natural for them to. But once here, it would seek something like the dark, tight places in which they dwell. Your boot was a handy option."

Ronan chuckled nervously. "Lucky me that I was the chosen one."

"Remarkably so," Alf agreed, "given that there were spots closer to the perimeter that would have served its purpose."

Tarben's expression turned hard, and he shared a look with Alf that was inscrutable to Ronan. "Let's move out. Now!" Then he took the boot from Alf's hand and knelt to put it on Ronan's foot himself.

* * * *

The hood of Ronan's cloak did little to stop the incessant rain from running down his face. Most of his journey into the Dark Mountains had apparently occurred during a dry respite from the bad weather. That luck had ended by the morning after the trip through the village, and as Tarben had predicted, the spritzing had increased to a deluge before midday. Ronan had been protected from the wet and cold as best as Tarben could manage, but they'd still spent a miserably wet night under a makeshift canopy of boughs. Remembering the snake in his boot from the previous morning, Ronan had kept them on. His socks got soaked, regardless. He was beyond ready for this wretched journey to end, no matter what fate awaited him.

As the Dark Mountains king's castle loomed in front of them, foreboding stole over Ronan, but there was also relief. This next leg of his ordeal was an uncertain one, but at least he'd be dry. As Tarben's horse brought him up to the guarded castle gates, however, he couldn't help feeling as if he was approaching his own tomb.

Tarben must have sensed his fear. Leaning over, he spoke into Ronan's ear. "I will keep you safe."

That reassurance should have meant nothing to him. Instead, it gave him a measure of courage once they'd stopped and dismounted. With his hand at the small of his back, Tarben steered him through the large open doors and into the anteroom of the castle. A handful of servants were there to greet them, meaning that they wordlessly took their dripping cloaks and Tarben's helmet. The clear sight of the man's face gave Ronan some comfort, as did Tarben's renewed contact as he led him through an archway and down the wide aisle of the throne room. There were courtiers lining the way, somber yet open in their curiosity. Ronan made sure to keep his back straight and his head held high. At the moment, he represented his country, and these Dark Mountains people needed to see the proud sureness of the Moorcondians—never mind that his legs felt weak and his stomach clenched with dread.

By subtle command, Tarben stopped them a short distance from the raised dais on which the king and his family sat. The man himself was an older version of Tarben, simple in his garb yet radiating strength. To his right, sitting on a smaller chair, was a younger man easily recognized as Tarben's brother. An empty seat of an even lesser standard was next to him. *That's where Tarben must sit.* On the king's other side was an older woman, handsome more than pretty, stern-looking but with a softness in her eyes as she stared at her son. And Tarben's sister likewise sat next to their mother, a toddler at her breast. Of all of them, she was the most outwardly friendly, a smile directed at *him*. The two women were nothing like his own female relatives, being modestly attired. Although they each wore elaborate jewelry, of sapphires and emeralds respectively, that Moorcondian court women would covet. It was an odd pairing with their simple clothing. A quick glance told him that the other women of court were much the same.

Tarben grabbed his attention by taking a knee and bowing his head. "My liege, I present you Ronan, prince of Moorcondia and my jarlina."

While he couldn't be sure, he sensed a ripple of relief run through the crowd. The king, however, showed no emotion. "You have done well, my son. Welcome to the Dark Mountains," the man added, his gaze shifting to Ronan.

It was hard to keep his head up and his eyes straight under the man's scrutiny. Ronan imagined how his brother would react under similar circumstances for courage. He didn't say anything in response to the king's words, either. They were mere formality. Everyone knew that Ronan was a captive, not a guest, and he wasn't going to make any of them rest easier by pretending otherwise. Their sensibilities were not his problem.

The Dark Mountains heir spoke up. "You will kneel before King Althelred!"

With his heart threatening to beat through his chest, Ronan answered as coolly as he could. "He's not *my* king."

The man rose from his chair with a snarl on his face and took one step toward the dais' risers. Before Ronan could think what to do, Tarben jumped to his feet and stepped in front of him, his hand on the hilt of his sword. "Stand down, Athur. I will not allow you to touch my wife."

The brother didn't like that one bit. His face declared his emotions easily. That was not a good thing in a future ruler. There was no chance for him to escalate the conflict, however, because the king intervened with a quick cut of his hand in both his sons' directions. Athur sat down, still glaring. Tarben let go of his sword and stepped back to Ronan's side. The renewed press of his hand on Ronan's back was surprisingly soothing.

The king motioned toward a man standing in front of the crowd. "Tanulf, send the courier with the missive about the prince's situation. Let us pray to the All Mother that this time, we are heard." The man, Tanulf, nodded respectfully, but he shot Ronan a look that made him uneasy and reminded him that except perhaps for Tarben, the people around him saw him as the enemy.

"Wait!" Ronan called out before he could think better of it. Beside him, Tarben grunted out a low sigh. All eyes were on Ronan now, making it hard for him to speak. He pushed through the fear. "I want to write a personal note to my father in my own hand…in aid of your cause. It will help more than a ransom demand."

The king's eyes narrowed. "*Offer* of a *treaty*."

"Call it what you will, my lord, but I can assure you that my father takes no more kindly to threats than you would."

"Then your life is forfeit," Athur spat out.

Tarben pressed his fingers into Ronan's back, the only outward sign of his feelings. He would have made a far better king than his brother because of that kind of control over himself alone. "You really need to remember that Ronan is my wife, brother."

Once again, King Althelred put a stop to the fight before it really began. "Enough!" He stared at Ronan. "What use would it be for you to do such a thing? Your father will only assume you did so at the point of a sword. *I* would," he added, throwing Ronan's words back in his face.

"There are expressions that I can use, codes if you will, that will convey to them that I speak in earnest. They will believe me when I say that I am well and that I truly want the treaty to move forward. I've seen the devastation to your people," he added in a softer tone, unsure of how well this king would take to being reminded that his people suffered.

"Or you can use that 'code' you speak off to betray vital information." This from Tanulf. The man was clearly an important member of the court to speak so freely. *He must be the cousin Tarben spoke of as being an advisor.*

Ronan directed his response to the king, however. This was the man who needed convincing, and Ronan was sincere in his offer. He hated knowing that these people were starving when his own country could help. His dreams had been haunted by the gaunt faces of the children in the village. "What could I possibly tell them that you won't? I have no idea how I got here or even where *'here'* is. I only know that we went through thick forests and along misty trails. My uncle, Prince Soren, could figure that out for himself. And I don't know how many warriors you have beyond the few that I've seen, although I can attest to their strength and skill. That's not going to prove useful to any action my uncle takes, either." He chanced taking a half step forward. "I truly want to help, my lord, no matter my fury and indignation over how I've been abducted." He said nothing about the forced marriage, as that was too mortifying. Everyone knew about it anyway, and who wouldn't assume that he resented it?

There was a silence as the king absorbed his words. Then, Tarben's sister broke it. "Father, I am inclined to believe him." She shot Ronan another smile as she tugged her bodice into place and cradled her sleeping child in her arms.

From what Tarben had told him about how the Dark Mountains were ruled, he expected the king to issue a rebuke. The man surprised him by turning in his daughter's direction and nodding. "Your counsel is always wise, Sari. What do you say, my dear?" He switched his gaze to the queen.

The woman didn't answer right away. She studied Ronan for a moment, her gaze assessing. Then, "I think that our son by marriage is in need of a warm bath after his long journey. Some food would also help, although I have no doubt that Tarben has been an attentive husband in that regard. After that and perhaps some rest, let us take this boy at his word and give him paper and ink." She shrugged. "Surely Tanulf is clever enough to spot anything amiss." Despite her words, she gave the mentioned man a dismissive glance.

The king nodded. "I accept the advice. Tarben, see to your jarlina's needs, then come and speak with me in my private chamber."

"Yes, sire." Tarben bowed once more before taking Ronan by the arm and hustling him out through a side door. The courtiers parted to let him through, still silent. Yet, Ronan could see by their expressions that they respected Tarben. And that was all to the good. In this place, Ronan would have to count on this man who claimed to be his husband to keep him safe.

* * * *

"Is the temperature to your liking, Jarlina?"

Ronan pried open his eyes in order to answer the boy. "Yes, it is perfect, thank you." He sank further into the warm water. It was doing an amazing job of chasing the chill from his body and easing the stiffness from so many days spent in the saddle. And the tub was big enough for him to straighten his legs — remarkable really, considering that the Dark Mountains didn't have indoor plumbing. The serving boy and his cadre had carried buckets of steaming water in from the gods knew where. Given the labor involved, he wouldn't have blamed them if he'd been given a barrel to soak in.

"It is my honor to serve, Jarlina. Is it your wish that I should bathe you?"

Ronan raised his eyebrows at the question. It had been a long time since anyone had helped him with such an intimate chore. And this boy was younger and even smaller than he was. It seemed like a laughable idea, except the servant was earnest in his question. Just when Ronan was about to dismiss him kindly, Tarben loomed in the doorway.

"I will see to the jarlina, boy. Go back to your daily tasks."

"Yes, Jarl." As he slipped past, Tarben reached out with his hand to ruffle the lad's hair. The fact that the servant didn't cringe at the sudden movement told Ronan everything he needed to know about Tarben. If the servants didn't fear him, he must be a good man...ordinarily.

"Your people like and trust you," he said once they were alone.

Tarben shrugged as he stepped into the small room and shut the door behind him. "I would like to think so." He sat heavily on a stool by the bathtub. His hair was wet, and he wore clean clothing. Given that this chamber was connected to the man's bedroom, Ronan had to assume he'd washed elsewhere and probably with less comfort. He looked enticing.

Ronan slunk deeper into the water, aware that his body was exposed, as was his sudden reaction to Tarben's presence. "Did you mean it about bathing me?" He held his breath waiting for the answer, not knowing which one he was hoping for.

Tarben shot him a smoldering look. "Would you like me to?"

"No!" Ronan folded his hands over his crotch to hide how much his dick disagreed with him.

Tarben said nothing, although his smile told the tale. He sat quietly, obviously not intending to leave while Ronan had his bath but not trying to engage him in any way, either. It took Ronan a little while to relax again. He closed his eyes and allowed himself to luxuriate in something as simple as a tub of warm water. By Moorcondian standards, this was hardly a noteworthy experience. The soap left for his use lacked a pleasant odor, and the wood of the tub was rough on his backside. Still, after so many days in the saddle and sleeping on the ground, his muscles practically screamed in relief.

"Do you wish to rest or eat first when you are done?"

Ronan's eyes popped open. He'd almost forgotten he wasn't alone. "Neither. I want to write that letter to my father."

"There is paper and quill in the bedroom waiting for you." Tarben paused and stared at him. "Do you truly want to help?"

Ronan was offended that the man had asked. After the time they'd spent together, he would have thought he'd know him better by now. "Of course I do. How could I not be moved by your people's plight?"

Tarben stared at the floor as he nodded. "Of course. I apologize for the question. It was insulting." He raised his gaze again. "Although our acquaintance has been short and brutal, I think I know you surprisingly well, Ronan. And you are a good man. Brave, too," he added with a quick smile.

It was hard to resist basking in the glow of such simple praise, not to mention the brief thrill of hearing his name on the man's lips. "I'm not sure I agree with your second point. I've been very meek in this adventure."

"You've been wise. There was no way for you to alter the course of our journey once I snatched you. A foolish man would have futilely fought, leaving me with no choice but to truss him up and sling him over my saddle for the duration. I'm selfish enough to be glad you didn't, because it would have left me feeling worse than I already do for my role in this."

Ronan gave the man an assessing look. "Do you really feel guilty?"

"I do. My whole life I have had only two things of note—my warrior skill and my honor. What I have done to you has left me with only one of those now."

Ronan believed that Tarben was sincere. Sympathy for the man's plight momentarily overtook his own self-pity. "I wouldn't say that. Not entirely. You've been kinder to me than the situation required."

"Because I didn't rape you or throw you to my men for their sport?"

Ronan's cheeks heated from more than the steamy water. He wasn't used to such frank talk, but that was exactly what he'd meant. "Yes." He lowered his gaze, surprisingly disappointed in himself for thinking such things about Tarben, however much the circumstances dictated it.

Tarben said nothing more for a while, then, "Are you steady enough on your own to get out of the tub, dry off and dress?"

Ronan merely nodded, not trusting his voice, afraid he might blurt out a 'no' and let Tarben help him with all those things. The temptation was strong and that scared him more than anything else had so far.

"I shall leave you to your privacy." With that, Tarben stood and strode out of the room, shutting the door behind him.

* * * *

Tarben paced his bedroom despite the fatigue he felt, as if he'd waged a long and hard campaign. But his body would not stay still whenever he sat, so he was forced to shake off the energy. The constant movement did nothing to ease the ache between his legs, however. Not even the climax he'd wrung out of his dick as he'd bathed had helped. His cock hadn't ever completely gone soft and was now as hard as ever. Seeing his wife sitting in the bathtub, steam rising around his beautiful face and skin glistening with drops of water, hadn't helped, either. His cock didn't want his hand. It wanted to sink into the tight heat of Ronan's ass. Nothing else would satisfy it…or him.

Huh, as if once would do anything. I want him now and forever. The strength of the feeling surprised him. No, not really. Ronan was exactly the kind of man he craved, delicate and vulnerable, yet mature enough to stand on his own when needed. The courage he'd shown in the throne room had both frightened him and made him proud. The king didn't tolerate being disrespected, but also admired fortitude. Somehow Ronan had managed to thread that needle, even though Tarben could feel how he shook inside. He'd ushered his wife out of the king's presence feeling as if they'd passed some unseen point in the whole horrid affair that made what he'd done more likely to succeed. Ronan might not embrace his role as Tarben's jarlina, but his concern for the Dark Mountains people and interest in helping was far more important. And Tarben was convinced of the boy's sincerity.

The bathing door opened, and Ronan stepped out. His hair was braided and draped over one shoulder. He was dressed in a simple tunic and trousers tucked into soft leather half-boots. It was nothing special, only the kind of clothing worn by boys of the court before they entered a profession or training as a warrior. They made Ronan look younger than Tarben knew he was. When the scheme to snatch the prince had been laid before him, Tarben had pictured someone much as he'd been at an even younger age. He'd assumed the prince would be a warrior, if not yet bloodied, at least sturdy and capable of protecting himself. Tarben had already killed his first brigand while patrolling the forest when he was a few years younger than Ronan was now, and he'd been tall and brawny to boot. It would have taken a few men to keep him in check for a similar journey as he'd taken Ronan on. Not that it would have been a good strategy. He'd meant what he'd said that Ronan had been both courageous and smart in how he'd acted.

The Moorcondian prince's strength was quiet, yet there and to be respected. At the moment, however, all Tarben could focus on was the boy's willowy frame and delicate features. His green eyes flashed with a continued defiance but also with something Tarben interpreted as an invitation. A challenge perhaps. No, that couldn't be. It was only his unruly dick that saw encouragement where there was none. As tempting as it was to go and gather his wife in his arms, Tarben was determined to hold on to his last shred of honor. He'd promised Ronan that he wouldn't even try to seduce him, let alone use force. He wouldn't falter, no matter the strength of the temptation now that they were both truly alone and only a few footsteps away from his bed.

Ronan ran his fingers down his braid. "You said paper and ink are here?"

Not trusting his voice, Tarben merely pointed at the small table near the fireplace. His wife walked to it, each step a study in grace. It was impossible not to track him and home in on the pert ass that was visible past the hem of the short tunic. And because it was so enticing, he forced himself to look away and cross over to the farthest corner of the room so that his wife was literally out of reach.

Ronan sat down and picking up the quill, dipped it in the ink well. He pursed his lips and stared at the wall for a moment or two before beginning to write. It took some time, Ronan obviously trying to get his words right. Tarben chose to look away, but each scratch of the quill's nub on the paper was like a scraping of his nerves. It was the only almost-tangible connection he had to the boy at the moment, given that he'd looked away and wasn't close enough to smell him. How ridiculous it was that his attention could be so consumed by such a mundane task. The answer was obvious. Everything that Ronan did, however ordinary, had become extraordinary in Tarben's mind. He realized with sudden clarity, that a life married to this man who rebuffed his touch would be a unique kind of torture.

"Here. Read this."

Tarben had been so lost in his own thoughts that he hadn't realized Ronan had finished the letter. "I don't need to."

"I want you to." Ronan held the paper out to him. "I am truly not trying to be deceitful and want you to tell me if you see anything that might be misconstrued."

Tarben approached his wife as he would a dangerous creature. Not that he feared what Ronan might do. It was himself that posed the problem. He took the paper from Ronan's fingers deftly enough that they never made contact. Then he read through the missive quickly. It wasn't in his nature to use words in a clever way. He was a straightforward man. So if there was any hidden message in what his wife had written, he didn't detect it.

"It appears in order to me."

"Good. Please take it to…whomever. I want the communication to my father to leave as soon as possible." Ronan folded his hands on his lap and stared at the desktop.

Tarben knew a dismissal when he saw it. Saying nothing, he turned and left his own room, feeling as if *he* were the interloper.

Chapter Six

Supper was a more lavish affair than they'd become used to. Tarben understood that it was his mother's way of welcoming Ronan into the family. A more self-absorbed person would have missed the nuance that, given the plight of the Dark Mountains, the meal of roasted fowl and vegetables with hearty bread slathered in honey and butter was a veritable feast. Even at court, his father didn't allow indulgence in food when so many went hungry that night. Ronan was aware of their plight and sympathetic. Despite what had certainly been a spoiled life as a prince, the boy made a point of complimenting the meal and thanking the queen for it. If his demeanor was subdued and aloof, it was to be expected. No one thought he would embrace his captivity gratefully, even if he was being afforded every respect that his station demanded. The tension as they ate was palpable, and it was with relief when his father called an end to the evening.

Tarben resisted the urge to touch his wife, even in small ways as he was tempted to do. Ronan didn't need his help and followed a half step behind him as they went back to his bedroom. *Our bedroom, now.* Not since leaving the nursery had he shared intimate space with another. His assignations, such as they'd been, had happened mostly elsewhere — the barracks, another man's quarters. This was his private room, and he didn't like sharing it with anyone. Well, he *hadn't* liked sharing it. Ronan's presence seemed like a completion, not an intrusion. It was a puzzling feeling, and he pondered it while Ronan made use of the garderobe beyond the bathing room. When the boy reappeared, wearing a simple woolen nightshirt and socks, Tarben's insistent arousal kicked into high gear. It seemed that it wouldn't matter what his wife looked like. He was always going to want him.

Tarben wordlessly left to see to his own ablutions, taking the opportunity to attend to his dick. It wasn't pleasurable. He grabbed the shaft with a punishing grip and jerked himself to a climax with legs braced and head thrown back. With his eyes closed, he could easily conjure up a picture of his lovely wife. He knew what Ronan looked like fully naked, thanks to the one river bath they'd been able to take. At the time, he'd forced himself not to stare, then the incident with the boulder had taken his attention. Still, it took no effort to relive the visions of Ronan's slender body with shapely legs, flat stomach and smooth chest. He wasn't like the hairy men of the Dark Mountains, and that alone made him exotic and desirable. And the feel of that silky soft skin as he'd held him in the aftermath of the boulder ordeal had made him want to stop touching and start licking. He still wanted to do that before turning his bride over and mounting that high, tight ass.

Samantha Cayto

Tarben came in a rush, biting back a groan and propping himself up with a hand against the stone wall. The orgasm left him gasping for breath and made his knees weak. His cock pulsed longer than usual as the orgasm emptied his balls. There had been a lot of pent-up need, given the lack of privacy on the journey home. His hand was drenched in his own cum, and once the pleasure started to wane, he felt foolish jerking off in the garderobe. He hadn't done that since becoming a warrior and now had done so twice in one day. Still, it was better than parading his need in front of his unwilling wife. No matter what, he didn't want Ronan to feel under assault in any way, however inadvertent.

He cleaned the remnants of his climax off his hand and dick, then washed his mouth and other places that tended to make him smellier than a sleeping partner would like. He wasn't so fastidious with his lovers, but those men were rarely different than he. He wondered if this was what men did before joining their wives in bed—not that he thought of Ronan as being female. How could he, given the sight of the boy's cock? Nevertheless, there was something about his wife that brought out the same instincts to pamper and protect that he felt with his mother and sister. It wasn't about their ability to take care of themselves, either. It was simply what he'd been taught was the proper conduct of a man.

He stripped down to his skin before returning to the bedroom. Fortunately, his cock was somewhat appeased and easily hidden by the folded pile of clothing that he held. Ronan was already under the covers, as close to the far side of the bed as he could get without rolling off it. He gave Tarben a cursory glance, then stared straight ahead, his hands clasped on top of what had to be his abdomen. Tarben's imagination let him consider that the pose was designed to hide the boy's own arousal. It was a nice thought, but he ruthlessly dismissed it. Even if some part of Ronan wanted him, too, there was no way he would act on it. Pride alone dictated that Ronan resist any temptation, especially given that ridiculous Moorcondian law about a marriage needing to be consummated. Having nothing useful to say, Tarben dropped his clothing on a chair and approached the bed.

"I trust you know that I will take no offense if you seek comfort elsewhere." Ronan eyed him briefly.

Tarben sighed, suddenly weary right down to his bones. "Yes, of course I do." Lifting the covers, he slid in beside his wife. He hadn't noticed while alone that the bed wasn't very wide. Despite his efforts to the contrary, his arm brushed against Ronan's. He tucked it behind his head to remedy the problem, pressing his elbow against the headboard. "But I won't disrespect you in that public way. If I lie with another man this night, everyone will know of it, no matter how discreet I am. What we do or not do in our marriage is our business alone."

"You make everything sounds so reasonable when it's nothing of the sort. I shouldn't be here at all, and you shouldn't be saddled with a wife who won't let you touch him."

"We have been over this ground before, Ronan. There is little for us to do other than our duty to king and country. What we want is of no matter to the more important issues at hand, except in this one way. No one can force us to do anything in this bed that we don't want." Rolling over, he added, "I am tired, and you must be as well. We can talk more in the morning if you wish."

He didn't state, however, that no matter what his needs might be, he wasn't going to leave Ronan alone any more than was necessary. It pained him to believe it, but the dangerous episodes on the journey back had him thinking that someone didn't want the treaty with Moorcondia to succeed. Even an accidental death of the prince would cause that nation to go to war with the Dark Mountains. There would be no other conceivable outcome.

It wasn't merely some disgruntled or misguided warriors who might pose the danger, either. Those men were not prized for their thinking outside of warfare. No, the manufactured accidents had to have been orchestrated by a man or men of higher authority — someone who lived in the king's castle. As much as the idea pained him, he couldn't see any other explanation — although to what end, he didn't know. His own imagination was no more complex than the average warrior's. Whatever was going on, he would keep his wife safe until the poison lurking within the court bubbled up for all to see. And because he had no way of knowing who was behind the plot, he had to keep his worries to himself for the moment.

With nothing to be done until morning, he closed his eyes and let go of his troubling thoughts.

* * * *

Tarben woke instantly in the way of all warriors, aware that there was something wrong. A strange, muted sound came from the far side of the bed, and it was so foreign to his ears that it took a moment to realize it was crying. *Ronan.* Tarben lay still, listening and trying to convince himself he was mistaken. But no, his wife was making the pitiable noise as quietly as he could. It cut through Tarben like a sword. When he turned his head, he saw the boy was lying on his side, facing away. His body shook slightly, another sign of his misery. A brief war raged inside Tarben before he rolled toward his wife and put a tentative hand on his shoulder. Ronan jerked at the touch but didn't otherwise try to shake him off.

Tarben took it as a sign that his comfort wouldn't be amiss. He slid closer, careful to keep his body from touching Ronan fully — not that he was hard. How could he be in the face of his wife's profound unhappiness? "I won't let any harm come to you." The words flew out of his mouth, even though he knew that they sounded hollow under the circumstances. He'd done little else but hurt his wife from the moment he'd kidnapped him.

He expected a furious rebuke, or at least an effort by Ronan to pull away from his hand. Instead, his wife turned over and threw himself against Tarben's chest. Then he clung to him, burying his face into the crook of his neck and crying no more loudly, yet with racking sobs. Tarben hesitated for only a second before wrapping his arms around him and holding him tightly. Tucking the boy's head under his chin, he stroked his hair in what he hoped was a soothing gesture. He wanted to add more words to his actions, but nothing useful came to him. It all sounded trite inside his head, so he stayed silent and let Ronan cry out his feelings.

Slowly, the shaking eased and the tears stopped flowing. Ronan tangled his fingers into Tarben's chest hair, not tugging, merely holding on. "I'm sorry," he whispered in a watery voice.

"For what?"

"Men aren't supposed to cry."

"They aren't?" He thought the Moorcondians must have many strange customs and rules. "I cried over the body of my boyhood friend when he was felled by the brigands we hunted in the woods. No one thought anything of it. Sadness is not a weakness."

Ronan was silent for a few moments. "How about fear? Men aren't supposed to be afraid."

Tarben couldn't help snorting. "I am beginning to believe that your tutors did you a disservice. Only a madman is unafraid. It's what you do despite those feelings that marks the kind of man you are."

Ronan shuddered on a deep breath. "Then I guess I'm the type who cries. Such a useless response… It solves nothing." He oddly snuggled closer, drying his tears on Tarben's chest. "I'm a coward."

Tarben felt instant umbrage at that observation. He tightened his hold before reminding himself he had to be careful not to make his wife more fearful. "You are no such thing. I admire how well you've handled this outrageous affront. You've never once cowered in my presence or tried to appease me. No one could have done more under the circumstances."

"My brother would have made it harder for you to carry out your plan, at least."

"Maybe so, but the outcome would have been the same."

"He wouldn't be clinging to you now, seeking comfort from the enemy."

Tarben sighed again and gave in to the temptation to kiss the top of Ronan's head. "You've reached your limit, that's all. The relative privacy of this night has given you an opportunity to vent your misery. And I am not your enemy — your abductor and captor, yes. But I don't wish you harm, and if there is a way to release you back to your people without hurting my own, I will find it." Even as he made the promise, something deep inside him rebelled against the idea of letting this boy go.

Ronan said nothing for a while. "I believe you are sincere, but I can't allow myself to feel hope. It hurts too much when it's dashed." Tarben wondered who had done that to him and wanted to rectify that situation with his fists. "I suppose I should appreciate that the gods at least sent me a man that I desire."

Those unexpected words caused Tarben's brain to scramble in an effort to take them in, although his dick understood all too well and responded in its predictable way. There was no chance of shifting to keep it from Ronan's notice, so he didn't try. Instead, he loosened his grip so that the boy could break free from his grasp if he so wanted. Gratifyingly, he made no effort to do so. To the contrary, with their bodies touching from head to toe, it was easy to detect that Ronan was also aroused. "Did they, now?" It didn't matter that these gods Ronan spoke of had no meaning to him. It was enough that Ronan saw their hand in their fates.

Ronan nodded and twirled his fingers more into Tarben's chest hair. "In Moorcondia, boys and girls seek pleasure with each other. It's a safe way to have fun without the consequences of making a baby. Many adults continue to do the same, even after they are married, although such infidelity is frowned on in my family. The idea of only wanting someone of your own sex is not really talked about. That's true, even though my great-grandmother has had a special female companion for many years, although obviously it didn't stop her from marrying a man and giving him heirs. I'm supposed to wed a woman," he added in a voice laced with new tears.

Tarben tightened his hug once more. "You don't want that." It wasn't a question because the answer was obvious.

"No. I want this." Ronan petted Tarben's chest much as he was doing to Ronan's head of hair. Then, he moved his hand to brush against the head of Tarben's cock.

The touch jolted him. His cock pulsed at the almost promise. His tongue felt thick, making it hard to speak. "A man."

Ronan nodded. "Yes, but not simply that. I have always dreamed of being just as I am now — cradled in the arms of a powerful soldier, someone I can feel safe with and who will care for me for the rest of my days." The boy let out a loud sob. "I should *hate* you. Why don't I?"

Tarben had no answer to that. He was simply too pleased to hear that it wasn't the case. After everything he'd done to Ronan, the young prince should despise him, yet in his most vulnerable state, he'd moved toward him, not away. Because he didn't want Ronan to feel badly about his actions, Tarben merely continued to hold him, not trying to persuade him that he should want him. Here, in the darkness of the night, this intimacy might be comforting. In the cold light of the new day, however, Ronan would likely regret it. Tarben didn't want to give him any more reason to by taking advantage of the boy's emotional state.

Ronan surprised him once again by clasping the shaft with a tentative grip and bucked his own erection against his hip. "Whenever I've dared pleasure myself, this is what I imagine." He played his fingers along the shaft, making Tarben's breath hitch. "A large cock, hard because I'm so enticing and a man eager to mount me with it. But if I give in to that temptation, I lose all chance of having our marriage annulled. Perhaps that's all for the best. I can't be what my family expects. Being a treaty bride for the rest of my life may be the most useful thing I can do for them."

Tarben pulled away from the boy just enough to tip his head back so that they could look each other in the eye. Even in the dim light of the banked fire, he could see the sheen of tears. "You sell yourself too short, and I will not bind you to me unless it's truly what you want." When Ronan opened his mouth, Tarben overrode what he thought he was going to say. "Now is not the time for you to make that decision."

Then Tarben took the liberty of claiming the boy's mouth. He'd intended to give a quick, reassuring peck. Once their lips touched, however, his passion took over. He lavished attention on his wife, tasting him all over before pressing for entrance with his tongue. Kissing was not something he did very often, his bed partners more interested in a quick climax than affection. He'd thought he wanted the same. No longer. He loved exploring Ronan's mouth, finding it sweet and welcoming. It was only when he sensed they both needed air that he broke it off.

Tarben tucked his wife's head under his chin once more to keep from assaulting him with another hungry kiss. He was breathless enough that talking was hard. "I will not mount you, but I can, however and only if you wish, ease your tension for this night at least." He made clear his meaning by sliding one hand down Ronan's hip, then rucking up the night shirt to expose Ronan's skin to his touch. It was so smooth and soft. He loved the feel of it, as he did the tight smallness of the boy's rump. Cupping the cheeks, he squeezed once before letting go. Then he moved to take Ronan's dick in his grasp. "Let me make you feel good. Please."

Ronan's answer came in the form of a sigh and a nod. And to make it even more clear, his grip on Tarben's cock tightened. Tarben didn't want the boy to do anything out of obligation, so he nudged that fist off his shaft as he grabbed both dicks in one hand. Although he was gentle in his tugging and tried to make the effort last, it only took a few jerks to send them both over the edge. Ronan cried out softly as his cum spurted over Tarben's hand, puffs of warm breath bathing the skin at the base of Tarben's throat. His whole body shook with the force of his orgasm, a delightful show of how well pleased he was with Tarben's efforts. His own climax was glorious, even in its simplicity. When they were both finally drained, Tarben gathered his wife as close as he could and kissed the top of his head.

"Sleep now. You are safe in my arms." *Even from me.* He now knew for a certainty how torturous it was going to be to lie with his wife, yet not be able to do what he wanted with more desperation than he'd thought possible. But he was a man of honor, and if there was a way to both keep his wife from harm and release him to his family, Tarben would find it.

* * * *

Ronan woke up, well-rested yet alone. As he lay staring up at the simple ceiling, he took stock of how he felt. The crying had broken the dam of emotion that he'd held inside during his journey into the heart of the Dark Mountains. Normally, it would leave him drained and sad. Not this time. If anything, he felt energized. A quick touch of his lips confirmed that they were puffy and sensitive from that amazing kiss Tarben had given him. His whole face was testimony to how their lips, chins and cheeks had rubbed against one another. It was a first for him, and he held the memory of the experience close to his heart. No matter what else happened in his life, he would cherish this remembrance, at least.

He rose to a sitting position with the covers pooled around his waist. A faint whiff of something he knew was cum wafted to his nose. The scent of it made his already engorged cock even harder. He was used to waking in such a state, but for the first time, it didn't bother him. After a night pressed against a man, his arousal seemed perfectly acceptable to him. And he knew that if he wanted, that same man would ease his need — not in a way that would preclude his return to Moorcondia but satisfying, nevertheless. There was no reason to expect that Tarben would show such restraint again, except yes, there was. Throughout the entire ordeal, Tarben had shown his nature through deeds as well as words. Ronan should hate and fear and mistrust him. He simply didn't, and he was tired of living his life in despair and self-loathing. It didn't matter what others expected for him to feel. As long as he was stuck in this place, he would at least take what pleasure there was to be had. There was no point in feeling guilty about it, either.

There was a scratch at the door. "Come in!"

The boy who had served him the previous night in the bath entered, a tray in his hands and a smile on his lips. Behind him there was a parade of other servants, lugging big steaming buckets. "Your pardon, Jarlina. I have something to break your fast, then you can bathe and dress for the day."

Ronan feared his cheeks were burning from embarrassment. Surely the others could detect what had occurred in the room the previous night. Then again, servants were used to such things. "Thank you." As the boy approached the bed, Ronan realized that he didn't know who he was exactly. "I'm sorry, I don't think I caught your name last night."

The servant seemed surprised to be asked. "I am Fren, Jarlina." He balanced the tray on Ronan's lap.

It was the perfect way for his erection to flag. The meal was simple — bread, cheese and dried fruit, along with some type of tea. "Thank you, Fren. But shouldn't I be eating with the rest of the family?" It was odd to refer to his jailers in such terms, yet they had gone out of their way to make him feel welcome the previous night. There was no reason to be rude. It wouldn't help the situation.

Fren chuckled. "Everyone has already eaten, Jarlina. It's mid-morning."

Ronan froze with his hand midway to his mug. "Oh! I had no idea." There were a few very narrow windows covered in heavy material. It was impossible to tell how high the sun was. "I'm not used to sleeping so late."

"The jarl gave strict instructions that you weren't to be disturbed before now."

"That was thoughtful of him." Tarben always seemed to know what he needed without having to ask.

It was a little disconcerting and yet also endearing. He'd always dreamed of a man who would be so for him. Too bad it turned out to be an enemy. *No, not that.* Tarben had said he wanted to protect him and give him a way back home. His words had rung true. Ronan knew the danger of hoping for something too much, yet couldn't help doing so.

He took a bite of bread and cheese and washed it down with tea. "Did the jarl say what I was supposed to do once I've eaten, washed and dressed?" Ronan wouldn't be surprised if he was expected to remain in this room all day, a prisoner in a comfortable cell.

Fren smiled brightly as more servants trooped in with buckets of water for the bath. "Oh, yes, Jarlina. The jarl asks for you to join him in the bailey so that he may show you around the palace. I have taken the liberty of airing out your cloak and boots."

Ronan dropped his gaze, mostly because he didn't want the boy to see how pleased he was that he was going to be exploring and not stuck in a chair all day. "Thank you. That was very kind."

"It was my pleasure, Jarlina. We all want you to be happy in your new home."

Looking up, Ronan saw an expression of such earnestness that he didn't have the heart to say that the Dark Mountains would never be his home. He wasn't even sure those words would have been the true.

* * * *

Ronan took in the view from the battlement, awed by the magnificent beauty of the Dark Mountains. This high up and with a bright day to illuminate the surrounding area, he could finally see the country with more clarity. "It's lovely." He stood close to Tarben with his cloak shielding him from the still-cool wind. It was the most relaxed he'd felt in days. "And I can see how impregnable your father's castle is. It could survive a siege forever, too, I'll wager. Was that the purpose of bringing me up here, to show me that my people can't mount a rescue?"

Tarben braced one shoulder against the stone and looked at him. "I wanted you to see this country through my eyes, that's all. This has always been my favorite place to come. When I was very young, my mother commanded that guards follow me to make sure I didn't lean too far over and plunge to my death. I was quite fearless as a boy."

Ronan flicked his gaze in his direction. "I'd say you still are. Stealing me off the streets of Moorcondia was a bold move." Stupidly, he instantly regretted his words, even though they were true, and he had every right to remain indignant over his kidnapping.

Tarben didn't move away. He kept staring at Ronan, which was both disconcerting and welcome. "I can't deny the truth of your words, although I am glad it was me and not someone else. A large part of my duty now is to care for you. I must say that pleases me."

Ronan rested his arms on the wall, then put his chin on them. "Does it?" He couldn't help remembering what the man had done to him in the middle of the night. The mere thought of it caused him to become aroused and embarrassed in equal measure. He was having a hard time looking Tarben in the eye.

"I believe I've been demonstrative about that." There was a smile to his tone, but his expression turned serious, and he leaned closer to Ronan as he spoke. "What happened to your face?"

Ronan's hand flew to one cheek, sure he was blushing. When he felt the roughness, he understood what the man was referring to. His answer really did make him flushed. "It's, um, nothing. Your…ah, beard I think roughed up my skin." When he'd seen himself in the mirror that morning, he'd felt marked. That sentiment didn't bother him as it should.

"Huh. My apologies, I wouldn't have expected that. I don't kiss other men very often and when I do, they usually also have beards, so…"

A ridiculous spurt of jealously overtook Ronan. "I suppose you've had an untold amount of lovers."

Tarben chuckled. "Well, it's true I haven't kept track of the number, but I am a man who tends to seek relief on a daily basis."

"We've been together for a number of days and you've gone without. Other than last night," he added, almost under his breath. Then he shot Tarben a look. "Unless you found relief on our journey here that I didn't notice."

Tarben's slow smile in response was so irritating that Ronan had a sudden urge to slap the man. "I did not. I would not disrespect my wife in such a way."

Ronan should really hate being referred to as that. Instead it sent a warmth through him that had nothing to do with sexual arousal. *What is wrong with me?* "I care not."

Tarben folded his arms. "Speaking of which…when I was being briefed about you, I was led to understand that you spent a great deal of time in the company of willing women."

Now Ronan's cheeks really did burn from embarrassment. "That's what I wanted people to think," he admitted, although if he'd kept up the pretense, perhaps Tarben would keep his distance. *Do I even want that?* "There are certain expectations for a man of my station, ones that I had no interest in meeting." Putting his chin on one palm, he turned his head to gaze at Tarben. "When my brother and I reached a certain age, ladies of the court started approaching us for assignations — all done with my father's approval, naturally. No one would have dared otherwise. Morlen was delighted for the opportunity. I begged off, saying I wasn't ready for it.

"It worked until we went to university. That's when I really started to feel the pressure to conform to how people saw me." He shrugged. "I decided that I could fool everyone so that they'd leave me alone. I don't want to lie with women," he added. "And I've been afraid to do so with men for fear that they'd see how much I crave them. I don't think my father would appreciate learning that overly much."

"You should not have to hide yourself." Tarben reached over to tuck a stray hair behind Ronan's ear. "You don't have to here. Come," he added, pushing away from the wall. "It's getting chilly."

With a last look at the scenery, Ronan followed Tarben to the stairs leading down from the roof. Before they got there, Athur arrived. He shot Ronan an angry look. "Surveilling our defenses?"

Before Ronan could muster a reply to the ridiculous question, Tarben intervened as he'd done the day before. "Do not disrespect my wife, brother."

Athur switched his attention to Tarben. "I think your head is turned by a pretty face, *brother*. Remember that he is no friend to this court."

"And whose fault is that?" Ronan spit out before he could think better of it.

Now Athur's piercing gaze was on him once more. "So you admit it's true, no matter the pretty words you put on paper."

Ronan stood his ground, refusing to be intimidated, and if Tarben's presence gave him the courage, then so be it. "I want to help the Dark Mountains people because it's the right thing to do. That doesn't mean I'm happy to have been kidnapped and forced into marriage."

"I don't think your wife likes you, Tarben," Athur sneered. "You'll have to do better in bed."

With hands clenched, Tarben took a half step forward. "You forget yourself."

"And *you* forget that I will one day be your king."

The two men squared off long enough that Ronan began to worry that he would be the cause of the brothers coming to blows. Then he reminded himself that none of this was his doing. What did it matter if two of his captors fought each other? Even as he thought it, his stomach clenched at the idea of Tarben coming to harm. As there was nothing he could do to control these powerful men, he tried to step away to at least avoid the coming fray. Tarben shot his hand out and pulled him over by his waist. He anchored him to his hip with a reassuring hug.

"Athur, I think you know that I am a simple warrior who is not one to use diplomatic words. All I'm trying to do is be the kind of husband that our father taught us to be. I will protect Ronan with my body if need be."

Some of the tension drained, including from Athur. "I know you will. I wouldn't expect anything less from you. But how about your wife?" He fixed his gaze on Ronan. "Are you truly married to my brother?"

Ronan could only give the one answer he had. "According to the laws of the Dark Mountains, I am."

Athur surprised him by laughing. "Ah, now *that* is a diplomatic answer, if ever I heard one." With that, he brushed past them and headed to the nearest warrior guarding the battlements.

"Have no fear of my brother, Ronan. He is still feeling his way as the heir and tends to be hot-headed."

Ronan gave no response because he didn't know what to say. He wasn't sure Tarben was right about that. There was an underlying feel of menace in that castle, and it was directed at him. All he could do was hope that Tarben really would protect him.

Chapter Seven

Ronan sat against pillows in Tarben's bed, twisting his fingers on top of the covers, as he nervously awaited the man coming out of the bathing room. After what they'd shared the previous night, he was conflicted about whether he wanted to keep his distance or not. If they could stick to pleasuring each other in ways that didn't constitute consummation of their marriage, this unsettling adventure just might be his one chance to enjoy another man's attention. Only pride stood in the way, and after bawling his eyes out in Tarben's arms, there seemed little point in trying to preserve *that*. He was already semi-hard with anticipation, although he hadn't dared to remove his nightshirt. Maybe Tarben would enjoy attending to that chore himself. The mere thought of the man undressing him raised goosebumps along his skin. Tarben appeared, gloriously nude and fully erect. He shot Ronan a smile as he approached the bed. The way his hard dick bobbed in front of him was mesmerizing. Ronan couldn't take his eyes off it, except something about the man's face did catch his attention.

"You shaved." Tarben's face was as naked as the rest of him, and for the first time, Ronan had a clear view of his rugged handsomeness.

Tarben stopped at the far side of the bed. "Yes."

"Why?" Ronan was trying to decide if he preferred the man with or without the beard, then decided he liked both equally. Which was disturbing because he shouldn't like him at all.

Tarben rubbed one thumb along his cheek. "It chafed you. I don't need it unless I'm outside for long periods of time during the cold season, so it's an easy way to protect you. Plenty of men do the same for their wives."

"Oh." Ronan wasn't sure how to respond to that. The consideration surprised him. "Thank you." He stared down at his twisting fingers. "Would you please leave the lamps turned up for a while?"

"If that is your wish." Tarben sat on the bed. "Why? Is there something you want to look at? I don't see a book in your hands."

Ronan heard the teasing tone. "I think you probably know the answer to that already. Would it be all right if I…um, explored your body?" He dared to glance at the man. The smugness in his expression was exasperating. Still, he had no one to blame but himself. "Not that I want to lead you on or anything."

Pulling his legs onto the bed, Tarben propped himself against the headboard. "I'm at your disposal, wife. I will give you anything you want and only that. I promised not to pressure you, remember?"

"Yes." Ronan dared to push aside the covers and twisted to kneel beside Tarben. "It's just that this is my first and maybe only chance to really study a man, to see how one is put together. I mean one that isn't me," he added with a grimace. "I'm nothing worth scrutinizing."

Tarben barked out a laugh. "Surely you jest. A more comely man I've never laid eyes on before. You are exceedingly beautiful, my jarlina."

Every time the jarl called him that, it sent a tingle through him, even though he should resent the title. "You are kind to say so, and I know that women and men find me attractive. It's just that I'm not interested in someone who looks like me. I much prefer your version of masculinity." He dared to look at the man from under his lashes, embarrassed but also hopeful.

Tarben held out his arms. "You may look...and touch, as much as you like. Consider me your plaything."

Oh, the invitation was too tempting to resist. Ronan only waged a short war within himself before giving in to what he wanted. He reached out tentatively to touch Tarben's biceps. The man's skin was a bit rough, quite warm and tautly hugged the rock-hard muscles. When he ran a finger along the hills and valleys, Tarben twitched and his nostrils flared. "Your arm is a big as my thigh."

"I need to be able to swing a sword." His voice was a low rumble that skittered down Ronan's spine.

Ronan dared to scoot closer, then continued his exploration by sliding his palm across Tarben's chest. The small thatch of hair nestled between his pecs was enticing. As he'd done before, he twined his fingers through it. "Moorcondian men rarely have this, which is a pity because it's so wonderfully manly." He dared to tug at a few strands. "Does this bother you, my playing with it, I mean?"

"Only in the sense that it arouses me." Tarben's chest rose and fell more rapidly and Ronan could swear he could detect the man's fast-beating heart.

A quick glance downward confirmed that the jarl's arousal hadn't abated and if anything, appeared harder. A small pearl of pre-cum welled up in the slit. Ronan licked his lips without thought before realizing his reaction might give Tarben ideas that Ronan was not yet ready to explore. Instead, he slid his palm over the ridges of the man's abdomen. The muscles rippled as he did so, and Tarben's cock bobbed, as if inviting attention. *It's too much. I can't.* Ronan snatched his hand back before immediately placing it on the thigh closest to him. If he turned tail now, he might lose his only opportunity to truly satisfy all his curiosity. He crept his fingers closer to the jarl's groin, stopped a moment, then clasped the shaft.

Breath exploded from Tarben's lips and his whole body jerked. "Yes, touch it. As much as you'd like."

Ronan didn't wait for more of an invitation. Rather, he concentrated on how Tarben's cock looked and felt. The skin was stretched so tightly that it appeared at risk of splitting open. It was different from the rest of the man's body, too…silky and almost hot. The hair surrounding it was even coarser than that on the chest. Nestled beneath the dick lay large balls. They looked full to bursting, except he knew that was fanciful thinking. Surely one could not detect such a thing, even though they must be ready to empty themselves. He gripped the shaft more firmly and could swear there was a pulse there, as if Tarben's heartbeat echoed within the cock. As Ronan played with it, moving his hand up and down, squeezing occasionally, Tarben's breathing became more labored and he clenched his hands.

"If you continue thusly, wife, I shall come in your hand."

Ronan understood that the jarl meant it as a warning, but he chose to take it as an invitation. He'd never watched another man as he climaxed, nor brought him to that state himself. It was impossible to fight the urge. So he jerked Tarben's cock as the man had done for him the night before. He knew his efforts were clumsy, no real rhythm to them, yet it only took a few passes before Tarben threw his head back on a bellow. Warm cum spurted from his cock, coating Ronan's fingers immediately. Rather than letting go, he stayed with this man who claimed to be his husband and watched as the ecstasy bathed his face, jerking his shaft until the last bit of cum left it. With his eyes closed, Tarben panted as if he'd run a great distance. Ronan carefully released the dick from his grasp, then gave in to another temptation. He raised his fingers to his lips and flicked his tongue out.

"Do you like the taste?"

Startled, Ronan dropped his hand and looked at Tarben, feeling like a child caught doing something naughty. He considered acting indignant, denying what he was so clearly doing. But that would have been cowardly, and he was tired of feeling that way. He lifted his chin. "Yes, actually. I rather do. It's a bit bitter, yet also salty. Shouldn't I like it?"

Tarben gave him a lazy smile while tucking one arm behind his head. "It can be an acquired taste. Many men — and women, I hear — don't. Others do. It is of no importance either way, although I'm glad that you enjoy mine." His gaze flicked down to Ronan's lap. "May I return the favor?"

Ronan didn't have to look to know what he was referring to. He instinctively pressed his hand to his lap, stifling his erection and soiling his nightshirt with Tarben's cum. "You need not."

Raising himself up on one elbow, Tarben's expression turned heated. "And what if I want to?"

"I-I suppose that would be all right." Ronan averted his gaze, too mortified by everything, no matter how amazing it had been. His breath left him in a gasp as Tarben whipped his nightshirt off him with a sudden, fast movement. Before he knew what was happening, Ronan found himself naked and on his back, the jarl lodged between his legs. "What are you doing?"

"I want to taste all of you—unless you don't want me to." The man's meaning became clear when he opened his mouth and lowered it toward the head of Ronan's dick.

"Oh!"

"Is that a yes, wife?"

Ronan nodded, words failing him. Rational thought fled the moment his cock was encased by Tarben's mouth. The man sucked his shaft all the way down, the base not being devoured because of the way Tarben's finger and thumb gripped it. An orgasm welled up and he clawed at the sheets in anticipation, only to be thwarted. A mewling sound escaped his lips before he could hold it back.

The jarl spit out the cock with a chuckle. "I don't want you to come too soon. It's better when you have to wait for it." So saying, he licked a stripe up the underside of the shaft before twirling his tongue around the head.

The sensations were all new and fantastically powerful. Ronan's own hand never produced this effect, and now he understood why other men got a wicked gleam in their eyes when they talked about blow jobs. The pleasure was exquisite. He was conflicted, wanting to experience the enjoyment of coming right away and delay it at the same time. He lay like a rag doll, quivering. When Tarben used his body to bend Ronan's legs and splay them open, he gave no resistance. Perhaps he shouldn't trust the man, but he did. There was a moment of tenseness at the touch of something wet against his exposed hole before he realized it was only Tarben's finger. It opened him enough to enter, a strange feeling of invasion, yet not painful. And when it scraped against something on the upper side of his channel, he gasped and groaned at the unexpected explosion of pleasure shooting through him.

Every breath became a laboring pant. He clenched his hole around the finger as it gently fucked him. Tarben sucked his cock all the way down this time. Nothing held back the climax. When he swallowed around the shaft, massaging every inch of it, Ronan came in a blinding rush. He shouted out his release, writhing and bucking in the jarl's hold. The intensity consumed him as nothing else ever had. He wanted it to last forever and, at the same time, couldn't bear it. No one had ever warned him that sex with another could be so overpowering. As he slowly came down from the high of it, he felt both exhausted and exhilarated and wanted to do it all over again. His fears of intimacy with another man washed away in the aftermath of the experience, he went unreservedly into Tarben's arms as the man gathered him close.

Tarben was delighted over how easily his reluctant wife melted into his embrace, even after the throes of his climax had abated. If he'd feared that Ronan would regret their lovemaking, he was reassured that in the dimness of their bedroom at night, that wasn't the case. What might happen in the cold light of day was another matter. But he wasn't one to borrow trouble. For now, he simply enjoyed this demonstration of trust and savored how hard he'd made Ronan come. He knew without asking that he'd been the first to do so, although likely he wouldn't be the last. The stray thought bothered him enough that he squeezed his wife more tightly.

Ronan grunted. "You're going to break a rib."

"Sorry." Tarben eased his hold and kissed the top of the boy's head. "Did I…hurt you in any other way?" It was a loaded question and one that wasn't necessary, yet he couldn't help asking.

Ronan snuggled closer. "I think you know you didn't. What you did to me was amazing."

"I'm glad to hear you think so."

"How could I not?" The little prince said nothing more for a while, so much so that Tarben thought he'd fallen asleep. "Do you think what you did with your finger means our marriage is consummated?"

Tarben hated the worry he heard in the question, although there was another emotion underlying it as well. Hope maybe? *No, thinking that way will lead to madness.* "Certainly not. Had I thought that, I wouldn't have done it. It was merely to enhance your climax. It worked, did it not?"

"So well it almost felt like I was dying."

Tarben chuckled. "Then I did my duty indeed." Once again, they fell into silence. He closed his eyes to let sleep claim him, but his wife wasn't done talking.

"Your brother hates me."

"No. He doesn't know you well enough to feel thusly. It's Moorcondia that he dislikes, because our entreaties were rebuffed. You are merely the symbol of that."

"I still don't believe that was my father's doing. It's not like him at all. Hopefully this new message, including mine, will reach him. I'm sure he'll agree to the treaty because he's a decent man and won't want to see your people starve if there is a way to help prevent it."

Tarben wasn't convinced. Children, even those of a king, often saw only the good in their parents. "I pray to the All Mother that it will be so. Athur has been skeptical of this entire scheme," he added, even though talking about the touchy subject with his wife was hardly conducive to a good relationship with him. There was something about lying in the dark, fresh from lovemaking, that loosened one's tongue. "He wanted to simply take what we needed through raids. It was our cousin, Tanulf, who came up with this idea."

Ronan huffed. "Well, they're both terrible plans. At least this one has some hope of a long-term solution to your problems. And I'd rather be the one suffering than see any of the outlying villages be pillaged."

Tarben winced at the stark assessment of the situation. "That's because you were born to serve your people and embrace that duty. We have that in common. Although right this moment, I don't feel that my duty clashes too much with my desires. You are lovely, wife, in all ways. I enjoy having you in my bed."

As soon as he'd made his confession, he held his breath, fearful that he'd gone too far.

"Right now, so do I."

He let his breath out slowly and ran a hand down Ronan's arm. "I'm glad of that. Now, we should seek our sleep."

"Okay," Ronan agreed in a tired voice and soon drifted off.

It took Tarben longer, his mind turning over everything that had happened. Someone hated his wife so much that they were trying to kill him. Of that, he was sure. Could it be Athur? He didn't want to think so, but no one was above suspicion, and Tarben would be damned if he allowed anyone to harm the lovely boy sleeping in his arms.

* * * *

It came as no surprise that Tarben headed toward the council meeting still buoyant over the most enjoyable time spent in bed with his wife the night before. More surprising was how much he liked the idea of leaving his wife still sleeping soundly. As a warrior, Tarben habitually got up with the sun, if not before it. Until his bringing Ronan home, never had he left someone tucked into his bed as he headed out to do his duty. It was surprisingly satisfactory knowing that while he labored, his wife rested safely. It was a form of caretaking that was unfamiliar to him, and it was pleasing. Ronan deserved the pampering, and after all the boy had been put through, it was the least Tarben could do. There was only an unrelenting worry about the boy's safety, but he had done the most he could by having his hand-picked guards stationed outside the bedroom door. It wasn't the same as standing there himself, yet would have to do. Tarben owed duty to his king and country, too.

He was the last to arrive at the council chamber. Everyone else was already seated at the large round table where the rulers of the Dark Mountains had gathered advice and made decisions for many generations. The worn wood testified to the history of his people more than anything else in the castle. All eyes trained on him as he went to take his seat next to Athur. His mother sat on the other side of his father, but his sister's place was empty. That surprised him. She rarely missed a meeting unless she was in the birthing bed. As it wouldn't do to keep his father waiting any longer, Tarben didn't ask any questions that were of no immediate importance to him anyway. He thanked the servant who brought him mead, bread and cheese and focused on the king.

The man waved at Tanulf. "Tell us."

His cousin inclined his head before speaking. "All is going according to plan, your majesty. I have word that your envoy has crossed over the Moorcondian border under a flag of truce."

Of course, going down the mountain was always faster than going up it. He and his men had made good time on their way to kidnap Ronan, after all, and the envoy had only two men with him. They must have ridden nearly non-stop, the matter being as urgent as it was. And those more clever than Tarben had long ago established a relay of communication stations. Each one in the chain would have lit a signal to convey the message without having to ride back. It was a crude system, yet useful for such occasions.

"And there was no sign of...*unpleasantness*?" This from his mother. She was a stern woman for the most part, never particularly affectionate, but she also had a kind heart that showed with this type of understated question.

"None, my queen. The smoke was white." Tanulf didn't have to tell anyone there that if the smoke had been red, that would have spelled a different outcome.

Tarben relaxed somewhat at the news. It wouldn't do to get overly hopeful so soon. Still, it was a good sign that the envoy and his entourage hadn't been killed outright. "What is your estimate of Moorcondia gathering its troops to the border?" He knew the answer. It had been discussed at length. For some reason, he needed to be reminded if only to ensure that he was close to Ronan when they learned for sure what the Moorcondian response would be.

Tanulf turned to him, his expression irritatingly patient. "As much as a fortnight, cousin. Nothing has occurred to change my expectations. Of course, the Moorcondians might surprise us and send only diplomats to negotiate a treaty."

Athur snorted. "Rubbish! Your runners will come to us with word of Soren leading his full complement of men right to our doorstep...figuratively speaking," he added when their mother's breath hitched. "We will never let them get this far. If they are stupid enough to invade, they'll die at the base of our mountains. Perhaps their rotting corpses will nourish our farmland."

Now their mother *tsk*ed in disapproval. The king patted her hand before rounding on Athur. "Such comments are not helpful." He re-focused on Tanulf.

"Do you wish to add more men to those waiting in the forest?"

Tanulf mulled the question before answering. "No, sire. I have no reason to second guess your wise decision of withholding a show of force unless we feel this effort will fail. I'm confident my men can retreat safely if it becomes necessary."

Tarben didn't dare consider what would happen if Moorcondia refused their offer of a treaty with aggression instead of diplomacy. Not that he could blame them. Kidnapping their prince had been an act of war, no matter the justification. He could only hope that King Auden cared enough about his son to at least grit his teeth and accept the distasteful option of bargaining with his enemy. The man had only himself to blame for this escalation. Tarben knew that to be true, and yet it brought him no comfort. No matter the provocation, everything his country had done and would do was a stain that only many generations passing would make fade.

"My men will be ready to launch our defense if need be." He provided the reassurance because that was his duty, even as he hoped that it wouldn't be necessary. If he met the Moorcondians in battle, Ronan would despise him for the rest of their lives. It shouldn't bother him one way or another, but it did. After the small lowering of the barrier between them, he couldn't help wanting to bring it crashing down completely. The mere thought of what he and his wife might do caused his cock to stir. He slammed back his mead to distract himself from the nascent arousal. This was hardly the place for *that* sort of thing, especially with his mother present.

"I pray to the All Mother that it won't," Tanulf said. "I remain confident that my suggestion, as distasteful as it has been, will work."

"Huh!" Athur drained his own cup before adding, "Now that I've seen the prince, I find it hard to imagine his father will care enough to meet our demands. As I think of it, he probably won't do more than send a token contingent of soldiers to die for the sake of national pride and nothing more. Why should he spill Moorcondian blood for that mewling thing?"

Tarben slammed his mug on the table with unintended force. Only a lifetime of training kept him from jumping to his feet and planting his fist in his brother's face. He longed for the days when they were young enough that such fighting would be tolerated by his parents. "I have warned you before, brother. You will show my wife the proper respect."

Athur gave him a dismissive look. "I suppose sleeping with the enemy has made it hard for you to remember who you are and who he is. No matter how sweet his…presence in your bed, if the Moorcondians react as I've warned, your jarlina will spend the rest of his days in the dungeon. That's assuming we don't deliver them his head in a sack."

"That is quite enough!" It was rare for his mother to raise her voice, but when she did, even the king was sufficiently cowed to not interfere. The man sat back in his chair, nursing his mug of mead and letting his wife cut their oldest to ribbons with her tongue. "This isn't some toy you are fighting with your brother over. Ronan is part of our family, no matter how he came to be or what he thinks he is. *No one* will harm him. He is innocent in this horrid situation. Never forget that.

"You will swear to the All Mother here and now that you will protect Ronan as you would any other vulnerable member of our family, no matter what." The queen leaned into the table, pinning her first born with a glare that still made Tarben shiver to see. It was having that same effect on Athur, who sat staring at her with wide eyes.

"I so swear, madam." Athur lowered his gaze. "I didn't mean to offend or upset you. My…my worry for our people made me choose my words poorly."

Their mother sat back. "That's one way of explaining it, I suppose. But your promise is sufficient to placate me. Please forgive my outburst, sire," she added with a glance to the king.

"You spoke for both of us, my dear." The king gave her an indulgent look that served as a quick unguarded moment to demonstrate his feelings.

Tarben had long known his parents loved each other. He'd never considered that he might make a similar match. It had never bothered him one way or another. Yet, sitting there, the memory of Ronan's sweet exploration of his body fresh in his mind, he couldn't help wondering if such a thing were possible for him, as well. *No.* As the talk continued around him, he was reminded that there were only two possible outcomes to this daring scheme. They might get their treaty, and the All Mother knew he hoped so, but then he would have to make good on finding a way for Ronan to return to Moorcondia. Or the situation could devolve into bloody war, infuriating Ronan to a degree he would never get over. Either way, his wife would be lost to him.

Chapter Eight

"Is there anything else you require, Jarlina?"

Ronan settled into his chair, full from his breakfast and clean from his bath. "No, thank you, Fren. I have everything I need." That wasn't entirely true. He knew without being told that he was confined to this bedroom until Tarben came to liberate him. *If* he did. The man was undoubtedly busy, too much so to pamper a wife who had been forced upon him. Although after the night they'd spent, perhaps Tarben had an incentive to return as quickly as possible. Ronan's cheeks heated at both the memories and the anticipation. He shouldn't be happy about getting close to his kidnapper and certainly he shouldn't be contemplating doing the kind of things they'd shared in the mostly dark during the light of day. It was unseemly. *Well, not really.* He wasn't so naïve as to have missed the various assignations that took place at all hours in the palace. Still, he didn't think it would be appropriate in these circumstances. *Pity.* His stiffening cock disagreed as well.

There was a scratch at the door at the right moment to distract him. Fren went to open it, then immediately bowed low when Tarben's sister sailed in with her infant snug against her shoulder and a maid trailing behind her. She smiled brightly at him. "I hope I'm not disturbing you."

Ronan jumped to his feet. "Not at all, madam." Tarben's sister was the least intimidating person in the man's family. Her visit was a welcome distraction, especially because he dared to hope the books the maid carried were perhaps for him.

And they were. Sari pointed to the small table near where Ronan sat. "Put them there." To Ronan, she added, "I thought you'd be in need of a diversion. I hope reading holds some appeal. It's either that or I can bring needlework for you to do." Her teasing smile made it impossible for Ronan to take offense.

"Such a lovely surprise. Thank you." Leaning forward, Ronan started sifting through the stack. They were mostly treatises on local flora and fauna, as well, as the history of the royal family and the building of the castle. One, however, titled *Tales from the Dark Mountains* appeared to be fiction. While he knew he should read the more useful books, that was the one he wanted to start with.

The jarlina sat in the chair on the other side of the fireplace and let her baby bounce on her lap. Ronan knew little of such things, but the child looked to be a few months old. It gurgled and grasped at Sari's beautiful ruby necklace. When the child started sucking on one of the gems, its mother seemed unperturbed. "She's starting to teethe already. You'd think that after seeing four other children through this stage, it wouldn't be so exciting. But it is, and that's especially so given that I've told my husband that she will be our last. I've done my part adding to my family."

Ronan wondered how the woman could be sure about being done with birthing babies. Perhaps she intended to keep her husband at arm's length. Then again, one of the books was about local medicine. The Dark Mountains women might have a solution to regulating procreation that his people didn't. Or it could be that the Moorcondians were equally adept, and he was simply ignorant of the process. That was certainly in the realm of possibility.

"You are a calm mother, indeed, to allow your baby to play with such a valuable necklace."

The woman looked at him with obvious confusion. "These are merely redstones—pretty but of no particular worth."

The answer surprised and confused him. Once again, he harkened back to his first fraught conversation with Tarben. The man had dismissed taking Ronan's own pendant as a bribe. His words had meant little at the time, and given how much his people needed food, it made no sense that the man hadn't at least sought to trade it for some amount.

Ronan stood and approached Sari. "May I have a closer look at it?"

The woman shrugged. "Certainly." She gently wrestled it away from her daughter's tight grasp and pulled it over her head. "I know it's a bit gaudy compared to our more sober way of dress, but it's the one particular indulgence of Dark Mountains women."

Ronan took the jewelry from her. "Thank you. I won't go far with it." He went to stand closer to the fire and tilted the gems in the light to get a better view of them. Not being well-versed in such matters, he nevertheless thought that he could tell if he were looking at rubies or not. *It can't be. Surely they would understand their worth and use them for trade.* Try as he might, he could find no obvious flaw in the gems. They appeared to be genuine and of no less quality that those his mother and other ladies of the court coveted. A thought occurred to him.

Returning to Sari, he both held out her necklace and pulled his own out from under his tunic. "May I ask you something? You have many of these stones as well, do you not?" He dangled his sapphire in front of her face, letting the firelight catch the reflection of the cut as best he could.

Sari handed her necklace back to the baby to gum. "Oh yes. You have bluestone, too? It's quite striking. Men don't wear jewelry here. Is it different in Moorcondia?"

Ronan returned his pendant to the place it always sat against his breastbone. "Yes. Men do, although really only members of my family as well as the nobility and wealthy merchants. How common are these stones here?"

Sari pursed her lips. "Common enough that you can find them at the base of the mountains, even without much mining. There are greenstones also, although the three different ones aren't near each other. It is my understanding that craftsmen tried to use them for tools, but they broke too easily to be useful." She shrugged. "They're simply pretty adornments."

"That is true in my country as well." Ronan went back to his chair and pondered this astounding information. He could be wrong. Lots of gemstones looked alike without being of the same rarity. What the Dark Mountains women wore could be little better than cut glass. He didn't dare voice his interest, however, not until he'd had a better chance to study them. "Is there bluestone to be found near the castle?"

"Hmm-mm." Sari bounced her daughter some more, a smile on her lips. "I'm sure if you're interested, Tarben would take you to see. There's nothing to be done while we wait for a response, after all." The woman's expression turned serious as she redirected her gaze back to him. "Please don't worry about that. Tarben will protect you, no matter the outcome."

"I believe you." He meant what he said. It might be folly to trust the man who had snatched him away from his home, yet he knew deep inside with certainty that Tarben was his protector. "I hope this turns out well for all of us."

And he might have found a path forward that solved all their problems — if he could convince his husband to indulge him on a little ride.

* * * *

"Thank you for this." Ronan guided his mount up the rocky slope.

Tarben rode slightly ahead of him to lead the way. "It's little enough given how cooped up you've been since arriving at my home. We still await word from the emissary, so I have nothing more pressing to do at the moment."

Left unspoken was that the situation could change at any time if Moorcondia responded to the overture by attacking the Dark Mountains. Not long ago, Ronan would have said he cared not what might happen to this man he was wed to if a battle ensued. He couldn't claim those feelings now. It hadn't taken much for him to grow close to Tarben, however much he'd fought it. Their physical intimacy hadn't been the catalyst, either. If he were honest with himself, he'd come to see Tarben more as a protector and ally then an enemy, even before he'd taken Ronan to his bed. It was important to him now to prevent a war between the countries for everyone's sake.

"I also appreciate being alone instead of having a contingent of guards surrounding me. Thank you for trusting me not to bolt."

Tarben shot him a quick grin over his shoulder. "I have come to appreciate that you are an honorable person, wife. You say you want to aid my people, and I believe you. Besides, I wouldn't need help catching you if you took off."

Ronan resisted the urge to stick his tongue out at the man. He wasn't a child, after all, although Tarben did manage to bring out the kind of reactions that Morlen used to when they had been young. "I happen to be an excellent rider. You make assumptions, *husband*, as to your abilities where I'm concerned." Perhaps baiting the warrior wasn't the best of ideas, but the day was lovely — warm and bright — and the air was fresh in these mountains, unlike in the city. He felt rather carefree.

"You do have an excellent seat, but alas, that pretty ladies' mount of yours would not outrun my warhorse for long."

Now Ronan did stick out his tongue, not by a lot, just enough to make himself feel a bit better. Then he kicked his horse to walk beside Tarben's. The path was sufficiently wide, and he could see that they were nearing an open area at the base of the mountain. He wondered if he should explain why he was asking to see a place where bluestones could be found. It was tempting, but he was still uncertain that he was right about the stones and he didn't want to get Tarben's, or anyone's hopes up. The Moorcondian royal jeweler had once shown him a variety of gems in their natural state, so he might be able to confirm his suspicions if he studied what he found. It was still a big question mark, however, so he kept his thoughts to himself.

As they entered the clearing, Tarben reined his horse to a stop. "Is this what you wanted to see?"

Ronan scoured the area, looking for signs of mining, however small. Spotting a likely hole, he said, "I think so, yes." He dismounted and held up his reins. "Would you hold this please?"

"Of course." Tarben was obviously curious about what Ronan was doing yet didn't ask. Maybe it was his warrior discipline. Ronan doubted he would be quite so reticent.

He walked over to the hole and first peered into it, then kneeled. Someone had dug down only shallowly. That was good, as he hadn't thought to bring a rope and doubted Tarben would be quite as complacent if Ronan asked to be lowered underground anyway. Besides, he really didn't like small spaces. Luckily, he spotted what he wanted, and it only required him to flatten on the ground and reach into the hole. He grabbed onto the rough bits of blue rock and pulled his arm back. Rising to his feet, he studied what he held. The bluestone was stuck to brown rock, yet he couldn't help getting excited. The jeweler had shown him sapphires in a more polished state than this and these stones were of a lighter color, but they did appear to be the real thing.

"Did you find what you were looking for?"

Ronan raised his head to answer. "Yes, thank you. We can return to the castle if you want."

Tarben glanced at the sky before saying, "That would be best. We won't lose the light for a while, but it will rain soon."

"Really?" Ronan tried to see what the man referred to and yes, there were ominous dark clouds on the horizon. He'd been lucky that the weather had held long enough for them to make the trip. "Let's go, then." He returned to his horse and mounted the short filly with ease. He tried not to feel too aggrieved that he'd been given a 'lady's horse'.

As Tarben turned his horse around, he said, "If you want pretty baubles, I am more than happy to gift you with them."

The comment startled Ronan. He'd been provided a fair amount of serviceable clothing since arriving at the king's seat of power. He was grateful to be able to remain clean and presentable, but he didn't think of them as gifts. It had never occurred to him to ask for any, either. Tarben's expression told him the man was serious in his offer, almost eager. Knowing that his husband cared about making him happy however he might under the circumstances warmed his heart whether he wanted it to or not. Other than his family members, no one had ever done such a thing. He couldn't hide his smile.

"That is kind, but my interest in these stones is more scientific that sartorial."

Tarben appeared disappointed by that answer. "As you wish. If you change your mind, I can get the royal jeweler to make something out of those. A ring, perhaps." He gave Ronan a sideways glance. "That is a thing in Moorcondia, is it not, for married couples?"

Ronan was tempted to make a retort about how they weren't really married. Something held his tongue, however. He didn't want to be mean to this man, given that he had no more say in the situation than Ronan did. "Yes, it is," he simply replied before kicking his horse into a trot. He wanted to get a closer look at the gems when he returned to his room — Tarben's room — their room? *Oh no.* Something had changed between them. The sex obviously had added intimacy but that was not the organ that controlled his emotions at the moment. He very much feared he'd grown fond of the man, so much so that leaving him no longer felt like the goal he wanted.

* * * *

Ronan stared at the stones in his hand as he followed Tarben through the labyrinth of halls to reach their bedroom. His concentration was such that he nearly bumped into Tanulf. Tarben reached out to pull him to his side. "Apologies, cousin."

Ronan looked up. "Yes, I'm sorry. I wasn't watching where I was going."

Tanulf treated him to what appeared to be an indulgent smile, yet didn't seem sincere in Ronan's estimation. "It is of no matter." He peered into Ronan's hand. "I see you've been gathering pretty stones." He turned his attention to Tarben. "Are you planning on giving your jarlina some jewelry?"

"If he wishes. For now, he is merely curious about them."

"Are you, Jarlina? How so, if I may ask?"

Ronan hid his keen interest for the same reason he had been doing so all along. He didn't want to raise false hopes that he'd found the perfect bargaining chip for the Dark Mountains people. "I've always had an interest in gems...no matter their rarity."

"I see. Well, I expect you need something to occupy your time. That reminds me, Tarben. The king has called you to his council room. I will be heading there shortly myself."

"As soon as I've escorted Ronan to our chamber, I shall hurry there."

Ronan put his hand on Tarben's arm. "There's no need. I can find my way from here."

Tarben narrowed his gaze at him, then stared down the hallway. "I suppose it is a straight and short journey at this point. I shall join you once my father has dismissed me." There was a certain heat showing through his eyes that did funny things to Ronan's belly and below.

"Okay," was all he managed to get out before hurrying on his way. For sure, he didn't want Tanulf to notice that he was aroused.

He nodded briefly at the guard waiting for him outside the door. This was one of Tarben's men, so he knew him by face if not by name. Seeing him there, Ronan realized with a start that it might be that the posted guards were not so much for keeping him in but for keeping others out. Why else would the man already be stationed there? Tarben would have been with him but for the unexpected summons. He wasn't sure how he felt about that possibility but resolved to ask Tarben when he arrived.

Ronan left the stones on the table by the fireplace before heading into the bathing chamber. He wanted to wash away the dirt of the ride and put on fresh clothes. There was enough water in the basin for him to take a sponge bath. He didn't want to inconvenience anyone by calling for hot water. When he slipped off his breaches, his cock disconcertingly sprang forward. For a moment, he considered taking care of that problem, then decided not to. It was fun to think of Tarben coming to him and tackling that chore. Ronan was sure Tarben would grant him that boon, and of course, Ronan would reciprocate in some manner. There were a few possibilities that wouldn't constitute a true consummation. He was surprised at how eager he felt.

Slipping on a robe, he padded back into the bedroom and over to the table. He picked up one of the stones and studied it against the light streaming through the window. It wasn't as bright as the outdoors had been, but now he had the time and opportunity to remove his necklace and compare both stones. The door opened behind him. "That was fast."

"Don't overtax that pretty brain of yours. It is indeed a sapphire."

Ronan's heart skipped a beat as he whirled around to look at Tanulf. "What are you doing here? And if you already know about the valuable riches of your country, why didn't you use them to bargain with Moorcondia? You must know how coveted they are by my people."

The smile the man shot him as he closed the door made Ronan's skin crawl. "I'm sure if you give it some thought, you'll have your answer." Tanulf started to walk toward him.

"You want them for yourself." It was obvious now. Tanulf was the one who did the trading for his king. He must have known for some time what he was sitting on. "You've let your people starve!"

Tanulf shrugged. "They're not *my* people. I'm not the king and never will be. Why should I rot away in these dismal mountains when there's a whole world out there I can explore with all the comfort that comes from being rich?"

Ronan's unease grew as the man got closer. He was trapped. The only way out was through Tanulf...or if he timed it right, he could scoot across the bed and outflank the man. "Why concoct this scheme of kidnapping me instead of fleeing with some gems?" He inched backward and closer to the bed.

"I don't intend to leave with only what I can carry in my purse. I have a whole wagon-full waiting for me and a few loyal men. We'll leave when everyone else is fighting for their lives."

"You want a war." The asshole's plan had become even clearer now.

"Of course. I expect the messenger who arrived a short time ago is bringing word to the king that your uncle and his army are amassing at the border. He arrived quicker than I expected but my plans are already set. I will be well gone by the time the fighting begins. I'm honestly not sure who will win — other than me, of course." The man stopped with Ronan just outside his reach. "You've proved harder to kill than I thought. A pity, but I don't suppose your being alive will stop your uncle from attacking. Pride demands no less, but your death would have given him an extra incentive to take no quarter."

Things clicked into place for Ronan. "The rock and the snake. Not accidents."

Tanulf shrugged. "Worth a try, and it wouldn't have mattered particularly if you hadn't been so observant about the gems. I underestimated you there."

Ronan tightened his fingers around the rough stone and his pendent. "Yes, you did." He threw them at Tanulf's face and leaped onto the bed. He was fast, but the Dark Mountains man was faster. By the time, Ronan had rolled off the other side, Tanulf had circled back and grabbed him by the waist.

Ronan opened his mouth to yell, but Tanulf clamped his hand over it. "There's no one to hear you shout, except the guard outside. Oh, but that's my man. Tarben's sickened moments ago. Something he drank, I believe. No matter. My man knows better than to disturb us. Removing his hand, he twirled Ronan around and slammed him face first over the side of the bed. Then Tanulf plastered himself against Ronan, grinding his obvious erection against Ronan's ass.

Ronan struggled as hard as he could, even knowing there was no way to best the larger, heavier man. "I will tell Tarben everything, and if you mean to kill me to prevent my doing so, know that he won't rest until he learns the truth." As he uttered the warning, he had no doubt of his words. Tarben would avenge him, but the idea of never seeing the man again made him sadder than the mere threat of death.

Tanulf leaned into him, his mouth close to Ronan's ear. "I'm not going to kill you. That would be stupid. Tarben has such a ridiculous sense of chivalry that you are right, he wouldn't stop until learning the truth of your murder. A betrayal by you is a different matter, however. You must have him awestruck with your pretty face if what I've heard is true. He should have breached your hole the very first night. Instead, he's left the decision in your hands. How noble of him…and stupid. Do you think he'll stay under your sway when he finds out that you offered up your ass to me first? He won't believe a word from your faithless mouth."

"No!" Ronan bucked against the heavy weight. Tanulf merely laughed, making Ronan's skin crawl and causing tears to threaten. But he wouldn't let them fall, because he would *not* give this bastard the satisfaction. Instead, he resisted with all his might as the fucker pushed aside Ronan's robe, exposing him to his groping hands.

"I shall be sure to prostrate myself at his feet, filled with remorse for yielding to your temptation. Whatever beating he gives me, yours will be worse. I doubt you'll have much chance to say anything, let alone convince him of your innocence." He slid his finger down the cleft of Ronan's ass and pressed his hole. "Hmm-mm. Very nice. I think I'm going to enjoy this unexpected chore."

Ronan clawed at the covers and yelled. Tanulf's weight bore down on him once more, making it hard to take in a deep breath. This time the man's hard dick slid between Ronan's cheeks. He closed his eyes, praying that it would be quick and that Tarben would believe him and not his cousin's lies. But why should he? Ronan was a reluctant bride, all but a stranger. Tanulf was family, and the man's treacherousness would become known too late to save him or the Dark Mountains people.

As he braced himself for the assault, the weight on his back suddenly lifted. Ronan could breathe freely. He lay panting for a moment or two before forcing his eyes open and rolling to his feet. Tanulf was on his ass against the far wall, with his half-hard dick hanging out. Tarben stood between them, his legs braced and chest heaving. The sight of his husband caused Ronin to sag in relief until Tanulf started talking.

He held out his hand. "Cousin, I beseech you. I have done you a terrible wrong but…" He shrugged with a smile. "I was weak, and the boy was very insistent. I know the marriage is one of convenience anyway, so…" Tanulf tucked his cock into his breaches as he slowly stood. "I apologize most sincerely for my transgression. Might I suggest you lock the slut away after a sound beating? That way he can't entice another as he did me."

Ronan glared at the asshole. "He's lying!"

Tarben held out his hand toward Ronan and only glanced in his direction. "Cover yourself." Ronan clasped the robe tightly around him, furious and frightened at the same time. Tarben wasn't going to believe him after all—not about this, anyway. Maybe he could still persuade him about the gems. It would be the surest way he had to return to his own people and try to pretend that none of this ever happened. Even as the thought it, however, he knew deep down he would never forget Tarben and what might have been between them.

Tarben focused his attention on Tanulf again before barking out, "Alf!"

The warrior opened the door and stood on its threshold. Behind him, a guard lay on the ground. "My lord?"

"You will bear witness." Tarben took a visible breath. "Jarl Tanulf, blood of my blood, you have dishonored my wife by putting your hands on him in violence and tarnishing his dignity. You will pay for this transgression with your life. Tomorrow at dawn, I will meet you in combat and defend my jarlina with my body."

Tanulf sputtered. "You can't be serious? I did no such thing. That slut offered himself to me."

Tarben took a step forward, his hands balled into fists. "Say that again and I'll cut you down here and now."

Tanulf's gaze swung around and landed on Ronan. The look of hatred and the promise of retribution made him shudder. "Very well, cousin. I will fight you, but I pity you for being duped into this. If it is in my power to spare your life, I will do so." The asshole had the audacity to look smug.

"I ask for no mercy and will show you none. This is your last night among the living. Don't you dare try to flee, either. I will hunt you down, no matter where you go."

Tanulf huffed out what might have been a laugh, but there was finally fear in his expression. He stormed out of the bedroom without saying another word. Alf followed, closing the door behind him. Then there was silence, or rather only the sounds of Tarben's harsh breaths. The man unfurled his fingers and approached Ronan, who knew a moment of almost terror before he looked deep into his husband's eyes. There was nothing to fear there. He met the man halfway and threw himself into his arms.

Tarben held him tightly. "It's all right. You're safe." He eased his grasp sufficiently to look him over. "Did he harm you?"

Ronan could only shake his head and lean into Tarben's embrace once more. With his ordeal over, he wanted to burst into tears. It wasn't dignity that held him back but duty. There was no time to wallow.

Tarben needed to know the whole of it because thousands of lives were at stake. They mattered far more than Ronan's sensibilities. And yet, he took for himself a little more comfort.

"He came in uninvited and attacked me before I could escape."

"Hush now. I knew the truth of it even before I entered this room to find him pinning you to the bed." There was a catch in Tarben's voice as if he, too, was holding back his emotions. "When Alf came to tell me that my guard had taken ill, I feared you were at risk. My gut has told me all along that someone was intent on killing you."

"You were so angry when you arrived," Ronan ventured, reliving his initial fear that Tarben would blame him.

"At him. At myself. Not you. I worried that if I let myself comfort you as I wanted, I would lose control and kill Tanulf right here. We have our ways to deal with this kind of thing. I want the entirety of the court to see by my combat that you were wronged." He shook his head. "I never suspected Tanulf of being behind your 'accidents' and can't fathom his reasoning."

Ronan reluctantly pulled away. "I can. Let me explain." He told Tarben the whole tale—about the nature of the gems and Tanulf's plan to start a war to hide his escape with the riches he'd hoarded. When he was done, he waited for a response. The one he got surprised him.

Without saying a word, Tarben enveloped him with his arms once more and claimed his mouth with a bruising kiss. The hard length of the man's cock pressed against him, but unlike with Tanulf, Ronan welcomed this sign that he was desired. Truth be told, his own dick had roused from the kiss alone. Tarben only released him when they both needed to take a breath.

Tarben still held onto him, their foreheads touching. "You are a marvel, wife. This news will save the people of the Dark Mountains. I'm sorry I thought you were merely passing the time with pretty baubles this afternoon. Forgive my underestimating you."

His words gave Ronan a sense of pride. "I didn't want to speak of it until I was sure."

"I understand. And I see now why you offered your pendent to me that first night. You dangled no doubt the price of a village's worth of food in front of my face, but I was too ignorant to understand that. We must tell my father."

Grabbing Ronan by the hand, Tarben started for the door, then stopped. "After you dress, of course." His gaze homed in on where Ronan's cock peeked out from the robe.

Ronan knew he blushed, but he also felt emboldened. He wanted to wash away the memory of Tanulf's assault and now knew that he wanted Tarben as he should. All of him. The consummation of the marriage didn't scare him as it had. As he stared into Tarben's dark eyes, he knew that he wanted to be able to do so...for the rest of his life? *Yes.* Against all reason, perhaps, he'd fallen in love with his husband.

Ronan tugged on Tarben's hand. "Take me to bed first, husband. Please. I want to give myself to you."

Heat flared in Tarben's eyes before he quickly banked it. "I can't tell you what those words mean to me, but I will not...cannot. I won't have you take a step you may regret because of heightened emotions — or, dare I say, because you think there will be no chance come the morrow?"

At first, Ronan didn't understand what he was saying. "What do you mean?" Then it became clear to him. "Oh! I'm not offering myself as some kind of gift before you die. I have every confidence in your skill, husband. However…must you fight? Can't the king merely throw Tanulf in the dungeons or something?" He meant what he'd said about Tarben's ability. Still, no one could know for sure what might happen in battle.

Tarben shook his head slowly. "I'm not killing him for his treachery to his king and country. I do this for you. And nothing you can say will dissuade me," he added when Ronan opened his mouth to do just that. "You are my wife, and I find myself inclined to give you whatever you wish within my power. Not this, however. I will avenge your honor because it is my duty. When the members of the court see my victory over Tanulf, they will accept it as a sign from the All Mother that you are innocent in his accusations.

"And it is the only way I know to quell this fury inside me over what he did to you. Now," he added with a smile, "let me ease your discomfort in some creative way, so that we can go tell the others the good news."

Tarben reached for him, and closing his eyes, Ronan tumbled into the safety of his strong arms.

Chapter Nine

It was a good day to do battle. The sky was overcast, so there would be no sun shining in his eyes, yet no rain fell, either. He wouldn't have to worry about water blurring his vision or his feet sliding in the mud. Tarben stood still as Alf strapped him into his armor. Tarben was calmer than he'd ever been before heading into warfare...and sharper. That was despite not having slept much. But he'd lain in bed with his wife in his arms and they'd come together many times in the dark to pleasure each other in all ways—save one. And that final act, the claiming of his wife, had been promised for this day. If that wasn't an incentive to win this personal combat with Tanulf, nothing was.

Ronan might change his mind. Yes, that was a possibility. The previous day had been fraught with high emotions. His wife might come to regret the offer. That was okay. Tarben had realized in that horrid moment when he'd seen his cousin pressing Ronan into the bed that nothing mattered to him more than giving the boy everything he wanted—even if that meant letting him go. The mere thought of it made him heartsick. And now was not the time to be distracted by such worries. He needed to focus on besting Tanulf. He was only sorry that Ronan would be watching. Despite Tarben's pleas to the contrary, Ronan had insisted that his place was here, supporting his husband. He had to admit that seeing his wife sitting with his family at the head of the proving ground behind the castle made him proud and more determined than ever to prevail.

Athur approached as Alf secured the last buckle. He gave Tarben the once-over. "You look as formidable as ever, brother. I have no doubt of the outcome of this trial by combat."

Tarben took his helmet and sword from Alf. "I appreciate the show of confidence, but as we know, the All Mother doesn't always do as we expect." He paused before staring hard at his brother. "I would ask for your promise that if things go against expectations that you will protect Ronan and see him safely returned to his people."

Athur dropped his gaze before answering. "That is a given, and you shouldn't have to ask such a thing. It's my fault that you do. I have not been as kind as I should have to your wife. I am sorry. And rest assured that my men have spent the night ferreting out Tanulf's conspirators. They've proven very cowardly and talkative. All Tanulf's emissaries were men in his pocket, paid to lie about Moorcondia's rebuffs, except for the last one. I don't have confirmation about it yet, but I believe that poor bastard was killed on Tanulf's command. Hopefully we'll get all the answers once we've rounded up the rest of them. Finding his treasure hoard will prove trickier, I fear. Tanulf seems to have kept that information to himself, which is a pity. It would be helpful to be able to approach the Moorcondians with a pile of gems already amassed to prove the truth of our offer."

"I'm sure every lady in the court would hand over her jewelry if it came to it."

"Agreed. My wife and daughters already gave me theirs in a sack last night, unasked. For the first time in a long while, they appeared truly happy and excited to contribute to the good of nation." Athur shook his head. "I can't believe it can be this simple after all our people have been through."

"I know. But even if Ronan were unreliable in what he thinks, we can be sure that Tanulf knew what he was about. The All Mother only knows how long he's held on to this information. Famine or not, he was always going to see to his own future and no one else's. The manufactured conflict with Moorcondia became merely cover for his theft." Tarben eyed his adversary across the field, ready for battle as he was. His hatred for the man would impede his judgment if he allowed it. He had to remain calm if he wanted to succeed.

Athur tracked his gaze. "Be careful, brother. Remember how sneaky he was when we played as children. He will do anything to win, although if he were smart, he would allow himself to die with dignity by your hand. Father will not be so merciful, I think."

There was no chance to reply as the herald sounded the horn to call the combatants to the field. A calm stole over him now, as it often did before he fought. He was confident in his skills and would not fail. The sight of Ronan sitting beside Sari, wrapped in a large cloak against the morning chill, reminded him again of the stakes. Instead of meeting Tanulf in front of the king, he strode over to his wife. Then he reached up to cup the boy by the back of his neck and pulled him close for a kiss that spoke what was in his heart. When he finally let him go, Ronan sat back with a stunned look on his face. Tarben winked at him before slamming on his helmet and turning into a warrior. He stood beside his cousin with his sword gripped tight and dangling by his leg while he waited for the king to give them permission to begin.

Althelred rose to address both them and the spectators who had gathered around the field. "These two men come before me to battle for the honor of Jarlina Tarben. I do not take this trial by combat lightly, especially as they are both of my blood. The challenge was made, however, in front of a witness, and what was agreed cannot be undone. May the All Mother protect he who possesses the true heart." With that, he sat once more and waved at the herald.

Tarben and Tanulf separated and squared off, waiting for the horn to signal they could begin. Tarben held his sword at the ready and took in then let out deep, slow breaths. As it always did as he faced another man, time seemed stop, and all the sights and sounds around him became muted. Every ounce of his concentration was on his opponent. He waited, letting Tanulf make the first move, as he knew the man would. Tanulf was sneaky, as Athur had reminded him, but he was also impatient. Tarben exploited that weakness. When the man lashed out with his sword, Tarben deflected it and stepped aside to cause Tanulf to overstep his mark. His cousin quickly recovered and to his credit, he didn't make that mistake again. He did make others, though, including trying to throw Tarben off balance emotionally by baiting him.

"Did you spend a pleasant night with your wife, cousin? I bet he still wouldn't give you access to his ass. Why should you die for him?"

Tarben knew better than to engage in that manner. Talking was a distraction while fighting. He couldn't afford to take his focus off the task at hand by hurling insults. Instead, he delivered a succession of heavy blows, feeling each impact of steel meeting steel right down to his bones. He almost relished the effect. It reminded him that he was in his element. There were few things he was as confident in as his fighting skills. Tanulf was good, but he'd elected to spend his adult life as an advisor, not as a warrior. His moves were rusty from disuse, and despite his bravado, sweat trickled down his face from more than mere exertion.

Sensing his advantage was growing, Tarben pressed it, forcing Tanulf to retreat. Tiring your adversary was a decent enough strategy, and he wanted to end the conflict quickly. There was no honor in toying with the man, and the longer this battle continued, the more likely Tarben himself might make a costly mistake. The world around him narrowed down to only the repetition of clashing swords and the dance the two of them made around the field. Tarben only saw his opponent and just heard the clanging of the steel and his own harsh breaths. His heart thudded with increased speed—not from fear, simply from the physical effort that went into battle, although his body wasn't being taxed nearly as much as it would have been with a stronger opponent. His confidence in victory increased with each blow. Tanulf was slowing, his movements becoming more clumsy. When he stumbled, Tarben pressed his advantage.

As Tarben swung his sword downward, aiming for Tanulf's neck, the man let go of his own, yet hurled himself into Tarben's legs. In the background of the constant murmuring of the onlookers muttering, one single voice—the sound of it having become a part of him—rang clear to Tarben's ears. *Knife!* He kicked at Tanulf's outstretched arm without even trying to see the truth of matter. At the same time, he pivoted out of reach and brought his sword down against Tanulf's helmet to tear it off his head. And with only a brief hesitation, he swung again to slice into his neck. It wasn't a clean beheading, but close enough that his cousin collapsed dead onto the ground.

Tarben stood over his adversary, gulping in air. Pulling off his own helmet, he wiped the sweat from his brow with the back of his arm. He tried to feel some sorrow for his kinsman and boyhood friend. Little arose within him. Tanulf's transgressions against not only Ronan but also his entire country had sealed his fate. And in the end, it was his hubris and stupidity that had caused him to try to discredit Ronan instead of fleeing the moment he feared his plan would be uncovered. If nothing else, Tarben had given the man a quick death without the misery of a public trial and execution.

He grunted when something careened into his side. No, *someone*. Ronan. Tarben dropped his sword in order to fully embrace his wife and simply stood there, not caring who saw, not really hearing the sudden cheers. All that mattered was the boy holding him close, softly crying into his shoulder. "There is no reason to cry, my love. I am victorious." He didn't even question his use of the endearment. It had been sitting on the tip of his tongue for days.

"I was so scared." Ronan's voice was muffled by Tarben's heavy clothing.

"The outcome was never in doubt. And...you did your part. I heard your warning as if it had been shouted into my ear."

"My Uncle Soren taught me that trick back when they still hoped I could make a good soldier. It's the first thing that came to mind when Tanulf went down in an obvious move."

Tarben kissed the side of Ronan's neck. "Was it?" He chuckled, the weight of the fight lifting from his shoulders. "Maybe we should have you train our warriors."

Ronan pulled back. "I'm just glad you listened to me."

"Always." Tarben was about to say more, confess what was in his heart, when Ronan gasped and pushed himself free of Tarben's embrace.

"You're injured!" Ronan stared at Tarben's leg while undoing his belt.

"Am I?" Tarben looked down and saw the red stain spreading around his thigh. It wasn't a mortal wound as he'd prevented Tanulf from sticking that point in the groin that could cause a man to quickly bleed out. It had been a near thing, however, and once again, Tarben's heart swelled with the knowledge that his wife had been looking out for him.

"He needs help!" Ronan shouted as he wrapped his belt around Tarben's thigh and yanked it tight.

Now the injury hurt. "Mother of us all!" Tarben roared and for a moment, the world winked out from the pain.

"Don't be such a baby," Ronan huffed. Standing, he added, "If you are a good boy for the healer, I'll be sure to make you feel much better."

The smile his wife sent him made Tarben's dick swell and his knees to go weak. The effect was only slightly marred when with a quiet sob, Ronan threw his arms around him and began weeping again.

* * * *

Tarben did his best to wipe away the dirt, grim and sweat of his battle with Tanulf. There was a bit of the man's gore on him as well, because it was near impossible to hack a man's head off without some backsplash. A bath was sorely needed in his estimation, because he wasn't going to climb into bed with his wife without being clean. But the healer had been emphatic that the thread sewn into his flesh to close his wound should not be made wet, so a soapy cloth would have to do. Perhaps it was just as well. Sitting in a tub of water might have driven him to taking care of the rampant hard-on that currently plagued him. That would not do. A quick release wasn't what he desired. He wanted Ronan, all of him, or as much as the boy was willing to give. Tarben was still not going to hold him to any promises made when his blood was up and his emotions running high.

But All Mother save him, he craved the opportunity to sink his cock into Ronan's ass with an intensity that could drive him mad if he ever gave it free rein. He was not going to do that, however. He wasn't even going to go into their bedroom with his erection leading the way, making unspoken demands. So he wrapped a thick towel around his middle and held it tightly to his body. The pressure against his dick made him wince. He paid it no mind, however, as he walked into the bedroom and found...Ronan. Lying on the bed. Naked. And aroused.

His wife shot him a coy look. "I was beginning to think you'd spend the rest of the day in there, that I'd have to shove a plate of the food that's been brought up for us under the door or something."

Tarben spared a glance at the table by the fireplace. It was laden with all kinds of stuff, no doubt because no one expected that he and his jarlina would be leaving this chamber for the rest of the day. They'd suffered a fraught morning and were not needed for anything by the king at the moment. Athur continued rooting out the traitors, and no word had arrived as of yet that the Moorcondians were in a position to be approached. There was nothing for Tarben to do. *Except fuck my wife.* The thought of it made his dick jerk against his belly. A hunger rose in him that had nothing to do with the veritable feast laid out for him on the table. No, this was for the one lying on his bed.

"I wanted to make myself presentable for you, wife." He whipped the towel off and dropped it on the floor. "As you can see, I'm quite recovered from my injury, as well."

Ronan's gaze lowered to stare at Tarben's cock – or rather he thought it did. His wife's words belied that assumption. "There is some blood seeping through the bandage around your wound."

Tarben moved his hand to obstruct that view. "It's nothing, the remnants of the healer's work. It's little more than a scratch. I've had worse, for certain."

Ronan huffed. "Why do fighting men always think it's a virtue to shrug off injuries? I've had paper cuts

Samantha Cayto

that hurt like a curse from the gods. Don't tell me that a knife wound doesn't bother you."

Tarben nodded once as he approached the bed. "You're right, it does. But I'm used to hurts and can't afford to let them slow me down. Duty calls, after all, whether I am injured or not."

"You're not on a campaign. It's all right for you to give yourself rest."

Tarben sat on the edge of the bed, facing his wife, careful not to get any closer for fear of losing control. His fingers itched with the need to grab, his lips tingled with the desire to kiss and his dick pulsed with the drive to sink itself into the warm tightness awaiting him. Maybe. Nothing indicated yet what his wife was offering. A man could dream, however.

He waved at his erection. "I doubt I'll be able to do so until this problem is tended to. Might you lend a hand...or something?" He smiled as he raised his eyebrows.

Ronan sat up with graceful motion. "I am likewise plagued as you can see. Come lie down beside me, husband, and let us see how we may help each other."

Tarben grinned more broadly. "I do love hearing you call me that."

"What? Husband?"

"Yes." His simple response did little to express what was truly in his heart.

Ronan twisted so that he was kneeling. "It's what you are, isn't it?"

"To me, yes. But I haven't forgotten that you came into this marriage with no consent." The thought of what he'd done to this lovely, kind boy made him sick with remorse. Regardless of Tanulf's perfidy, that would never justify or excuse what the Dark Mountains people and Tarben in particular had visited upon the innocent Moorcondian prince. No matter what happened this day, Tarben vowed he would return Ronan to his home if that was what he wanted, even though it would crush Tarben to do so.

Ronan ran his fingers through strands of his hair and lowered his gaze. "I don't think that matters anymore. However much anger and resentment I've felt, it doesn't change what I feel now." He lifted his chin to look at Tarben once more. "I want you more than anything, and that feeling started before this morning or even yesterday. We've been heading toward sealing our marriage for some time now, even though I didn't want to admit it."

Tarben dared to reach out a hand and lay it on his wife's knee. "Whatever we do in this bed, it will remain between the two of us. No one has to know that Moorcondian law has been satisfied." He choked before getting out the next words. "I will deliver you to your uncle and declare our marriage void."

"You would dishonor yourself by lying?"

"I would lie to protect someone for whom I am responsible. Your safety and happiness are more important than anything about me."

"I see." Ronan shifted once more so that Tarben's hand got closer to the boy's shaft. "And what if this is what I want?" He swept his hand to encompass everything around them, including themselves. "To have a man make me his for the rest of my life, to provide for me and do battle in my defense if need be? Someone who would love me, perhaps.

"I've always dreamed of such a thing," he continued, once again with his eyes cast down. "Our tutors used to make my brother and me read about

148

Moorcondian history. We read stories of the days of old, brutal ones often, tales of bravery and forging our country into what it is today. Morlen loved the ones about battles fought and won, the strategy behind it, the cunning victories and the newly created weaponry. I read those, too, of course. It was expected of me. But when I was alone, I reveled in the history of how our family came to be. I liked reading about brave, strong men sweeping women into their arms and keeping them happy and safe for the rest of their lives. Not that there was many of them and not a lot of detail. History is written by men, primarily, so of course they had not much interest in telling about such things. And I suppose much of it was untrue. Politics forge marriages, not love."

Tarben moved closer when his wife went silent. "One does not preclude the other. I believe my parents love each other."

"I know mine do." Ronan lifted his head on a shuddering breath. "Is it wrong for me to want such a life? Does it make me less than a man?"

"Oh, my darling wife, of course it doesn't." Unable to keep his distance any longer, Tarben pulled Ronan into a tight embrace and kissed him with the kind of passion he hadn't dared show before. Without asking for permission, he invaded Ronan's mouth with his tongue and tangled it with his. Everything about the boy was warm, silky and welcoming. He tumbled them down flat on the mattress, reveling in how their aroused cocks rubbed against each other. That contact alone would soon send him over the edge.

His urgent plan was thwarted when Ronan pushed against him with more strength than Tarben would have thought he could. It was Tarben, then, who landed on his back, staring up at his wife. "Did I hurt you?"

Ronan rolled his eyes. "Of course not. It's *I* who don't want to harm *you*." He punctuated his point rubbing his fingertip along Tarben's bandage.

Grabbing the boy by the waist, Tarben tried to wrestle him back down. "Fortunately, passion is an amazing painkiller."

Ronan swatted him away. "I don't want to know how you learned that—and it doesn't matter, regardless. We will do this my way."

Enjoying his wife's spirit, Tarben dropped his hands and relaxed into his pillow. "I am yours to do with as you wish, wife."

"Good." Ronan scooted over to his side of the bed and reached over the edge.

The sight of his small rump in the air nearly drove Tarben mad. "You are the worst kind of torturer."

"Huh?" Ronan sat back on his heels. "Oh. Men are such simple creatures, myself included." He held up a small pot. "I'm merely ensuring that you have easy access to my body without causing me undue discomfort."

Tarben's breath stuttered. "You prepared."

"I want to be pampered, but I'm not helpless." He fluttered his eyelashes at Tarben, showing him a side of himself that he'd never seen before. "Now, lie still. I'm going to do all the work."

Tarben did as told, lacing his fingers behind his head in order to ensure that he not give in to the temptation of taking control. He wasn't sure what his wife had in mind, but it hardly mattered, as anything and everything would bring him great pleasure. What mattered was that it was Ronan in his bed. Tarben wanted no other.

It started out slowly, maddeningly so. The boy began with peppering Tarben's face with soft, gently paced kisses that eventually landed on his lips. Everything was light, with Ronan not lingering long on any particular place. Tarben tried to encourage his wife to claim his mouth more aggressively but was frustratingly ignored. He had to tighten his grip on his laced fingers to remain passive. Ronan understood what he was doing because he flashed a teasing smile before venturing farther south on Tarben's body.

"Do you find this a sensitive spot?" Ronan asked right before he twirled his tongue around one nipple. When Tarben arched into the touch, the boy hummed. "I guess you do." He wasted no time giving the other one some attention. Then he alternated between the two, tangling his fingers into the hair between Tarben's pecs, and tugging on it at the same time. When he scraped his teeth along one of the raised nubs, Tarben couldn't hold back the cry.

"You are a quick study, wife," he said between gritted teeth.

"I've always been good in the classroom." He demonstrated the truth of his claim by licking a trail down Tarben's chest and belly that stopped at the head of his cock.

Tarben's muscles quivered uncontrollably, and he held his breath as he waited to see what Ronan would do next. He was not disappointed. With only the briefest of pauses, the boy sucked the dick in. As big as Tarben was, not much of his cock fit inside his wife's small mouth. It hardly mattered. It was the motion that counted, and as inexperienced as the boy was, he still enthusiastically laved and sucked what he could. It was too much.

Placing one hand on Ronan's head, Tarben said, "Please stop. You'll make me come too soon."

Ronan pulled off the dick and sat back on his heels. His lips were shiny from the effort, and his expression was positively wanton. He was enjoying himself as much as Tarben was and seeing that washed away the last vestiges of doubt about what his wife truly wanted.

"We can't have that." So saying, Ronan picked up the pot once more. He dipped two fingers into it and scooped out some of the thick cream inside. "Fren swears by this concoction."

"You discussed sex with a servant?" Tarben wasn't embarrassed for himself, but he hated the idea that Ronan might be.

But the boy simply shrugged. "It was either ask him or your sister. Whom would you have preferred?"

"Oh. When you put it that way…"

Ronan proceeded to slather the stuff on Tarben's cock. It was hard to keep himself in check as those fingers danced along his shaft. He wanted to urge his wife to great speed and only held his tongue because it was obvious how important it was for Ronan to be in charge. It made sense, naturally. What would happen next in this bed would be monumental to the boy, and his deflowering had to be done carefully. Handing him control was an excellent plan and one he wished he'd thought of himself.

Once Tarben's cock was fully slicked, Ronan pushed off from his heels and reached around to his ass with more cream on his fingers. Although Tarben couldn't see his wife prepping his own hole, he could imagine it. Undoubtedly the boy was inserting first one finger, then two, pressing the cream in while stretching his puckered ring. The images made his dick jump, and he couldn't hold back a groan. That got him a knowing grin from his wife, and Tarben would have happily waited for a long time for Ronan to be ready. But the boy finished quickly and straddling Tarben's hips, positioned himself over his cock.

"Wait!" Tarben grabbed Ronan's waist to hold him steady. "That's not enough. I'm a large man, wife. I don't want to hurt you."

Ronan shook his head. "I can't wait. Not any more now that I know what pleasure can be had with another man. And I want to *feel* it, Tarben. The memory of your claiming me is something I want to treasure for the rest of my life...*our* lives," he corrected before he sat on Tarben's dick.

The journey through Ronan's snug, hot channel was a slow yet unstoppable one. Tarben felt every bit of the tightness wrapped around his dick. His wife's expression told him that he also did. With his eyes half closed and his mouth set in a straight line of concentration, Ronan told the tale of being breached. It had to be causing him some amount of discomfort, but at no point did Tarben register that his wife was in any real pain. Certainly Ronan's own erection didn't flag. And All Mother be praised, the pleasure was too great for Tarben to worry over it, in any event. He closed his eyes and melted into the mattress.

When Ronan bottomed out, he sat still on Tarben's pelvis. The boy's hole spasmed around the base of Tarben's dick, and his body quivered. Opening his eyes only enough to see, Tarben scrutinized his wife's face once more. Ronan stared back at him, silent yet with obvious determination. Then he began to ride. The pace wasn't quick at first but gained speed as Ronan no doubt became more acclimated to the shaft lodged in his ass and more confident in his movements. Soon, he was bouncing on Tarben's lap with abandon. Tarben knew he wouldn't last much longer, so he clasped his wife's cock and jerked him in rhythm to the fucking. When the climax came, he bucked up into his wife and knew the greatest joy of his life as they both cried out. He continued to milk Ronan's cock, cum splashing over his fingers, until the boy stopped moving.

They ended up tangled in each other, lying face-to-face and panting from their exertion. Tarben forced his eyes open to look at his wife, because he, too, wanted to remember this experience for the rest of his life. The thought of that somehow not including Ronan struck a sudden fear in his heart. Gathering the boy even closer, he bared his soul before he could talk himself out of it. "I love you."

Ronan squeezed him before saying, "Good, because I love you, too. I'm where I always dreamed of being — with a great man who has claimed me for his own. I belong to you, Tarben. It is my greatest pleasure to be known as your wife. Your jarlina."

Emotion clogged Tarben's throat. He had to push his words past it. Ronan deserved no less than a vow in equal measure. "I will care for and protect you for the rest of my life, and I will give you whatever is in my power, especially when we lie here in our bed."

Ronan kissed his shoulder. "Good, because I want you to fuck me. Now, if you can."

Tarben laughed before rolling his wife onto his back. "I will always be ready for you." With that, he pushed Ronan's legs apart and, finding his hole, breached it with one long push. It was just as tight and welcoming as it had been the first time. Only now, Tarben was in control, and on hearing his wife's pretty moan, he began to thrust.

No matter how hard Tarben fucked him, Ronan's cries of pleasure only increased. He clutched at Tarben's back, scratching his skin and bucking his hips to meet Tarben's dick with equal force. The second orgasm was no less intense than the first, and as he emptied himself inside the boy's ass, Tarben knew for a certainty that he could never give him up.

Chapter Ten

Ronan's ass ached as he entered King Althelred's
council room. The feeling was a familiar one now and
something he reveled in. His dreams had come true,
and the whole experience being new, he couldn't get
enough of it. He was so happy that he wanted to wear
a big grin on his face all the time, letting everyone know
his feelings and confirming that he and his husband
had finally consummated their marriage. It might not
mean anything to the Dark Mountains people, but it
did to him. He was Tarben's now and would never
argue to the contrary. If his family became angry at the
news, he would deal with it. Somehow, he would find
a way to reassure them that this was what he wanted.

He was careful to show a more sober face, however.
News had come that a herald had arrived this morning.
The king had sent for Tarben and Ronan both, which
was either a good sign or bad. He was sure his uncle
must have arrived at the border of the two countries,
although what had actually transpired was something
he was apparently about to learn. Soren was a decent

and temperate man. Surely he was there to talk first and not simply invade. If nothing else, Ronan was certain his family didn't want to jeopardize his life if it could be avoided.

The king waved them over to a large table covered in a map. Tarben tightened his grip on Ronan's hand as they approached. "What news, sire?"

It was Athur who pointed his finger to the river that lay between the two countries. "Prince Soren has made camp as close to the water as possible without actually going into it. His point has been made. He is ready to enter the Dark Mountains at any time."

Ronan wanted to ask questions yet knew his place. He needed to let his husband handle this for the both of them. "Has there been any talk between him and our emissary?"

"Only in that Soren has demanded that he see his nephew before any negotiations will take place," Athur answered.

Tarben snorted. "He wants me to place my wife between two armies?"

"We cannot be surprised by that," the king interjected. "He wants proof of life. And we'll give it to him, along with a bag of gems to demonstrate the truth of our offer." Athelred tossed a large purse on the table. "We found Tanulf's stash. The stones in there are polished sufficiently that their nature should be obvious, even to an untrained eye."

Ronan couldn't hold his tongue any longer. "I will assure them that it is so."

Tarben tugged him closer. "You will have no opportunity, my love. I'll let him see you from afar but will not put you close to anyone's sword."

Ronan frowned. While he was determined to be a biddable wife, he couldn't stay silent if he knew his husband was making a mistake. "I know my uncle, and he will not be satisfied by only seeing me waving from across the river. He'll require assurances from me that I am not harmed. And I can confirm that I consummated our marriage of my own volition." This last statement made him blush before he continued. "I can also assure him that there are more gems in the Dark Mountains than are in that purse. I'm the only one who can."

Tarben cupped his face and stared into his eyes. Ronan could see the love and worry in his. "I know what you say makes sense, wife, but it chills me to the bone thinking of you caught up in a battle. All it takes is one rash warrior to start it off."

Ronan squeezed his hand. "I know, but please let me do this for you — for all of you. For all of *us*. The Dark Mountains are my home, too, after all."

"Your jarlina is very wise," the king said. "Listen to him, then obey me. You leave as soon as you can make ready."

Ronan smiled for the first time since entering the room. "It won't be a long journey. I can ride my horse this time, and we won't need to rest as much as we did on the way here now that you know I'm not so delicate. And it will be all downhill, will it not?"

"Yes," Tarben answered on a resigned huff. "There is that. You will stick close to me, though, wife, and obey me without question. If I tell you to bolt, you bolt. Understood?"

Ronan batted his eyelashes. "Yes, Jarl."

* * * *

Ronan was exhausted. It was embarrassing to have weathered the journey more poorly than he'd expected. Tarben had set a brutal pace, and Ronan had managed to keep up for a long time before he started falling asleep in his saddle. That was when Tarben had transferred him to his warhorse, keeping him safe within his arms as he'd done on the way to the castle. Truth be told, he was happier traveling thusly. It had given him a chance to get some rest without slowing them down. And Tarben's arms were the most comforting place he knew. Now the river was in sight, and it caused his heart to tighten when he saw the Moorcondia banner flapping in the breeze beyond it. Not long ago, it would have bolstered his hope of being set free. Now, it reminded him of how dangerous matters were for his husband and both their peoples.

He straightened. "I should change over to my own horse."

Tarben's arm tightened around him. "Why?"

"It will reassure Soren to see me on my own and not encased in your embrace." He turned his head to look at his husband. "As lovely as it is."

Tarben looked down his nose plate at him, as he'd done the first time. "I would wish that we were only enjoying a day's ride to a sunny meadow. It scares me more than anything that you are surrounded by so many brutal men who are ready to wage bloody war."

There was truth to the man's words. Ronan could estimate from his childhood lessons how many Moorcondian soldiers camped across the border, and Tarben had brought a sizable amount of warriors, with more to join them shortly. If there was to be war, the men of the Dark Mountains had to defend their people, even though this had been of their king's making.

"I'm scared, too, but also hopeful. I have to try to make this right and save lives on both sides. If the worst happens, my life will be no more important than any other."

"And that is where we disagree, wife." Regardless of his words, Tarben helped him dismount and signaled for someone to bring Ronan's horse forward.

This one was sturdier than the filly he'd ridden before. It wasn't a real warhorse, because he would have had trouble handling something so big, yet it had weathered the journey well enough. When Ronan settled himself in the saddle, he felt confident that the creature was up for whatever he demanded. He stood facing the river.

Tarben pulled up beside him. He had removed his helmet, but his sword still hung from his belt. "Your uncle arrives." That fact was clear. Soren's standard was on full display as he walked his horse to the edge of the riverbank. There were only a handful of men with him, ready to defend their prince, yet not being provocative.

"I would like to get closer with only you and Alf, if you please. I know my uncle, and he's trying to demonstrate that he's not spoiling for a fight."

Tarben took a deep breath, then let it out on a rush. "Alf!" When his right-hand man arrived, Tarben motioned for the three of them to move forward. "I trust you in this, wife. If you are wrong and suffer for it, I will be quite cross."

Ronan couldn't hold back his grin. "Fair enough, husband."

As they walked their mounts toward the river, Ronan was careful with his expression. It would be hard to tell from this distance yet, but he wanted to be sure that his uncle saw nothing but calm resolve on his part. He kept his head held high, as well, to signal that he was not beaten down or ashamed. There would be time enough to tell the entire story at some point. For now, let his demeanor proclaim to all that he was a proud Moorcondian prince and that no one held a knife to his throat or a sword at his back. Tarben, he noted, was careful to stay abreast of him so that his hands were visible, and Alf was well to the side. They pulled their horses to a stop at the muddy bank.

Ronan lifted his hand in greeting and waited until his uncle did the same before lowering it again. The waters of the river were calmer than when he'd been taken across that fateful night. Even so, it would be very difficult to hold a conversation over its noise. It was ridiculous to even try. He turned his head slightly to speak to Tarben. "We need to go over there if we are to make any headway in these negotiations."

"No."

Ronan grimaced. "We can't very well shout at the top of our lungs to each other."

"True. I will go. You will wait here." Tarben kicked his horse forward and waded into the river.

Ronan's heart squeezed with sudden fear. *What if Soren has him killed while making a dash to get me?* He was not going to take that chance. He knew with certainty that there was no danger to him from his own people. Tarben was fair game, however, especially if Soren assumed the Dark Mountains warrior had brutalized him during the kidnapping. Without giving it any more thought, he followed his husband into the water before Alf could stop him. The warrior was not to be dissuaded, however, going in after him. And now Ronan had two men to worry about. *I have to reach Soren first.* With a forceful kick of his heels, he sent his horse cantering, passing his husband, who was making his approach slowly to show he meant no harm.

"Ronan!" Tarben's roar shook the mountains.

There was no stopping Ronan, however, until he arrived at the opposite bank. He was brought up short by his husband catching him and grabbing his reins. The look on the man's face as he leaned over to Ronan was fierce. "I have never hit a weaker person in my life, but I swear that I will take a belt to *your* pretty rump for this disobedience."

A perverse thrill ran up Ronan's spine. He had the presence of mind, though, to hold up his hand to his uncle. "I am well!" To Tarben, he said in a low voice, "When we have accomplished what we must, I will accept my punishment, husband, with good grace. So long as you fuck me afterward."

Tarben's face turned a dark red and he grimaced, but his pupils were blown wide, a sure sign that the man was aroused. As was Ronan, although there was nothing to be done about it at the moment. Tarben settled back in his saddle, yet kept his hold on Ronan's reins. "Let's go talk to your uncle."

It was a matter of a very short ride to get within arms' length of Soren. The man wore an almost amused expression. "Nephew, you seem well." That wry tone helped Ronan relax a bit.

"I am, thank you. May I introduce my husband, Jarl Tarben of the Dark Mountains. His father is King Athelred, and we are here as his emissaries."

Soren looked from one to the other of them. "Your husband? We were informed of it in the missive sent by King Athelred, but we were skeptical of its veracity."

"It is the truth." Ronan kept his tone firm and kept his gaze steady. "We were married by the laws of the Dark Mountains and…it has been consummated." Tarben uttered a sound that was part sigh, part groan of frustration. Ronan paid him no mind. "I am here freely to plead the case for a treaty."

"Are you now?" Soren no longer sounded amused. "And with what—other than your body—are these people intending to bargain with?"

"This." Ronan held out his hand, sure that Tarben would give him what he wanted. Once the heavy purse hit his palm, Ronan tossed it to Sir Rolf.

His uncle's man pulled open the strings and peered inside. "Gems, your grace. Big ones."

"That's merely a sample. The Dark Mountains are filled with sapphires, rubies and emeralds, enough to keep the denizens of my father's palace giddy with delight for many years to come. And in exchange, they ask for only one thing in return…food. They're starving, Uncle Soren."

Soren glanced from the purse back to Ronan. "I'm going to need more of an explanation."

"And you shall have one. Let us retire to your tent and talk."

"Very well."

"You're not going alone." Tarben's voice was practically a growl.

Turning to him, Ronan reached out to clasp his arm. "Please, husband. I will be safe. You know this to be true, and I can't have a frank discussion with my uncle with you hovering over my shoulder. He'll never believe in my sincerity unless he's sure you can't intimidate me. Trust me," he added in a lower tone. "I love you, and nothing will keep me from returning to your side."

Tarben stared back at him silently for a while before taking his hand in his and pressing his lips against the back of Ronan's fingers. "I do trust you, wife, and you know what's in my heart, as well, by now. That is why it's so hard for me to let you leave my sight. But you are right in this. I know you are, so I promise to wait right here, and I'll do nothing to cause these soldiers of your uncle's to express their hatred for me with the point of a sword. Come back soon, however. I am not a patient man."

"I disagree with you there. If you weren't, I wouldn't have been able to fall in love with you. Thank you for this." He reluctantly pulled his hand back and walked his horse toward his uncle. "Shall we?"

* * * *

"You need not poke at me so, Uncle." Ronan squirmed out of the man's grasp and put some distance between them. The tent was large, so it was easy to do.

"I merely seek to confirm for myself that you are unharmed. Perhaps I should send for the healer."

"You will do no such thing! I'm fine, other than being tired from the fast journey we took to get here." He walked over to a chair. "Do you mind if I sit?"

"You are the son of the Moorcondian king and can do as you like."

Ronan flopped down. "I am keenly aware of my station, given the circumstances."

"I'm sure." Soren went to the other chair and sat, staring at him intently. "And apparently you are wedded to the son of the ruler of the Dark Mountains. That makes you a prince twice over."

"He's the second son."

"That does not surprise me, given that you would have a hard time delivering the man an heir."

"And he's styled as 'jarl'. I'm known as his jarlina." The title had rankled at first, of course. Now he took pride in it. "Jarlina Tarben...kind of like Princess Soren."

Soren winced. "Taryn hates being called that." With a sigh, he stared at Ronan as if he were trying to see into his soul. "Are you truly well?"

"I am. Tarben has been kind to me."

Soren raised his eyebrows. "You mean other than the kidnapping and what I assume was a forced marriage?"

Ronan tried not to squirm. "Yes, other than that. And," he said before being asked, "the consummation part was entirely voluntary."

"Was it now? I wouldn't have thought that a captive had that kind of agency over his own body. Abductors usually get their own way. I understand, too, how consent can be a muddy thing when treaties are at stake."

Ronan was sure that his uncle spoke from his own experience, but this situation was different. "Well, I did have a choice, because that's the kind of honorable man I am married to. Tarben only did what his father commanded, and that was because they thought Moorcondia had turned them away when they needed a trading treaty the most. Plus," he added rather grudgingly if he were being honest, "consummation isn't required under their law for a marriage to be valid."

"But it is under ours. You understand what you've done?"

"Naturally." Ronan blinked rapidly against sudden tears. Tiredness and the high emotions this meeting brought on threatened to overwhelm him. It was critical, however, that his uncle not think he was at all wavering in his decisions or that he was suffering from some kind of duress. He trained his gaze on Soren. "I fought him at first. Of course, I did."

"I'm not suggesting otherwise." His uncle's tone was kindly and his expression sympathetic. It was not surprising. Ronan had never feared his family would blame him for this or turn their backs on him as a lost cause.

"He was respectful, apologetic even, but he would not be dissuaded from marrying me and bringing me to his father's castle as a hostage. It all made no sense until I saw the state of the Dark Mountains people. That's when their desperate circumstances became known to me. After that, I was an ally in their scheme, but I held on to the hope of being returned to my family with the marriage annulled."

"Then why, dear nephew, have you made that impossible? You can still come home, of course, but you'll be tied to that man for the rest of your life – or his, actually." Now there was a musing tone to his uncle's voice.

Ronan leaned forward. "You will not harm him!"

"Calm yourself. I didn't say I would."

"You were thinking it, though, were you not?" When his uncle gave him a rueful look, fear shot through him. "Hear me well on this, Uncle. I love Tarben. Offering to help his people was easy. You would have done the same. What happened after that was driven by my heart and nothing more. I want a treaty between our nations, and both will benefit, I assure you. My future with Tarben is a separate matter."

"Very well. We'll table that issue for the moment. Tell me how this whole situation came about. The Dark Mountains never approached us for a treaty, so their abduction of you and insistence on us coming to the negotiation table came as a surprise, to say the least."

Now that they were talking about the political and not the personal, Ronan felt more at ease. "I know that now, as does the Dark Mountains king. This awful situation was born from a scheme by a traitorous family member. Now that everything is out in the open, I'm truly hopeful that we can help these people."

"This sounds like a long story. Let me get us some wine, and you can tell me all of it."

* * * *

"It's hard to believe they didn't know they were sitting on a fortune's worth of gems."

Ronan blinked at his uncle through sleepy eyes. The fatigue of the journey was catching up to him. He wanted nothing more than to lie down. "They have lived isolated lives for untold generations. From what I read of their history, the population came together from various other countries, including Moorcondia, because their settlers wanted a quiet life apart from what they were leaving behind. They have written a lot of stories about it and pride themselves on their independence from other nations. Very few of them ventured across their borders to trade. The royal family was grateful that Tanulf wanted to do so.

"I had to help them. You see that, don't you? Any of us in the royal family would have done the same as I if they'd seen those starving people...*children*."

"I'm sure that's true. We were all raised to be compassionate."

Ronan drained his glass of wine, then yawned loudly. "Sorry. I'm exhausted."

Soren plucked the goblet from his lax fingers. "Yes, you are. Whether you realize it or not, you've been engaged in a kind of battle since your abduction. A long sleep somewhere safe is what you need most right now. My pallet is at your disposal."

The offer was very tempting. Ronan yawned again. "I must go back to Tarben. He'll be worried."

Soren stood. "You are solicitous of him."

"I love him." When his uncle tugged him to his feet, he went willingly.

"So you've said, and I believe you." Soren led him over to the pallet and gently eased him onto it. "Your father and I have always known you were...different. Unlike me, you were never destined to lead soldiers. An advisory role was the obvious choice, except we also knew that court life wouldn't suit you, either. It was clear to us, as well, that finding a wife wasn't going to please you." He helped Ronan lie down on his back.

Oh, this was so very comfortable. He could happily stay there for the rest of the day, so long as Tarben was with him. His uncle's words penetrated the fog in his brain. "How could you know what was in my heart when I didn't dare think of it myself?"

Soren pulled a soft blanket over his lower half. "It seemed obvious to anyone with eyes who bothered to look carefully. All those beautiful ladies of the court being turned away was an enormous clue. And Igon's and Sir Frauk's reports of your activities while at university confirmed it. A young man in your position could have amassed dozens of lovers, yet you spent every night alone in your bed."

Ronan forced his heavy eyelids open. "Oh, Sir Frauk! Is he well?"

"Other than trying to turn in his resignation every day, he is fine."

"It wasn't his fault. Tarben and his men are huge. He didn't stand a chance against them." Visions of Tarben flashed in his head, reminding him again how much he'd desired the man right from the beginning. He wanted him now and always, which made him realize anew that he wasn't with him. Ronan tried to sit up. "I must go to my husband."

His uncle eased him back down with the press of his palm. "Be still, nephew. I will fetch him for you. You are safe…and so is he."

"All right." With the reassurance, his resistance to sleep evaporated and he let it take him under.

* * * *

Tarben had been trained as a warrior to fight under the cover of the woods. He knew how to remain quiet and still for many hours. He understood the reward that came from patience. And yet, sitting atop his horse, waiting for his wife to reappear, every fiber of his being screamed at him to charge through the Moorcondian encampment, find the boy and race him back across the border—where he'd be safe, where Tarben could protect him from harm for the rest of their lives. The rational part of him knew it was ridiculous to fear for Ronan. He was surely in no danger with his uncle…unless the Moorcondians thought him a traitor for giving himself to the enemy. Might they be trying him with execution in mind this very moment as Tarben sat with his thumb up his ass?

Stop it! I am no good to anyone if I let my imagination run wild. Such was the effect of love, he supposed. Having never intended to feel such a sentiment for another man, he hadn't thought about it. Sitting there, gazing unwaveringly in the direction his wife had ridden off in, he could see how it might be seen as a kind of madness. How else could one describe his overactive imagination or the way in which his body was in constant motion in small ways that could only be described as fidgeting? He hadn't done so since childhood when he'd chafed against his tutor's boring lessons. Surely others must see his growing distress, even as he tried to hide it. His horse certainly detected it, becoming restless in response to its master's nervous energy.

Then it all changed in an instant. Prince Soren came into view, trotting toward him. There was a moment of relief before panic threatened to overwhelm him. Ronan was nowhere to be seen. Tarben started toward the prince before the man arrived. "Where is my wife?" He didn't care that his question — uttered in a roar — caused heads to turn and hands to go toward sword hilts.

Soren pulled up in front of him, both man and horse annoyingly calm. "Sleeping in my tent." His reasonable tone grated on Tarben's nerves.

"Without me by his side? I don't think so. Ronan would never." It didn't surprise him how certain he was of this. He'd seen what was in his jarlina's heart and didn't question it.

Soren inclined his head. "In all honesty, I helped him along with a mild potion."

"You drugged my wife!" His horse snorted and pranced at his fury.

Once again, the Moorcondians made ready to defend their prince. Soren held out his hand to hold them back. "He was exhausted, anyone could see that, and far too concerned with the treaty and you to allow himself to simply let go. I make no apology for what I did. He's given me the whole tale of how we ended up here, as well. So his duty to you and the Dark Mountains people has been fulfilled."

Before Tarben could respond, Soren motioned to a man that had stuck to his side the same as Alf did for him. "Your grace?"

"Have the quartermaster requisition what food stuffs we have and can afford to lose before re-supplying and prepare them to be handed over to the Dark Mountains warriors across the river." To Tarben he said, "I understand some of your villages are near enough that what we give you can be delivered relatively quickly. I offer this as a gesture of my confidence that a treaty can be made in short order between our countries."

Because he was dedicated to his people first and foremost, Tarben banked his anger. "On behalf of my father, King Athelred, I thank you. Anything you can spare will be most welcome." He waited until the prince's man left, shouting the prince's orders before speaking again. "Now, take me to my wife before I tear through this fucking camp to find him!"

Chapter Eleven

"As you can see, Ronan is perfectly fine."

Tarben didn't spare Soren a glance. His gaze remained fixed on his sleeping wife. Ronan lay on his side, facing him, his hand tucked under his cheek and looking more peaceful than he'd ever seen him before. He dared to reach out and brush some strands of hair away from his cheek. "He is the most beautiful creature I've ever laid eyes on."

Embarrassed at laying bare his emotions in front of another warrior such as himself, he stood and worked to return to his stern demeanor. That's when he realized that his wife was naked under the blanket. He whirled on his *host*. "Who removed his clothes?"

"My pages." Soren's calm was irritating under the circumstances. He acted as if Tarben were the irrational one. "Boys no older than Ronan and very efficient. My nephew needed a wash. And so, frankly, do you. Which is why…"

Two boys entered, wearing the passive expressions of good servants doing their jobs. They brought a large jug and bowl with them, plus a few towels and a pot of what he assumed was soap. They put it all on a table, poured water into the bowl from the pitcher and left the tent without so much as a glance in his direction.

Soren waved at the offering. "Please feel free to avail yourself while we talk. Once we're done, you are welcome to join Ronan on my pallet." Oh, the man was crafty, understanding that Tarben wanted to do just that and had no wish to lie beside his wife in his current dirty and smelly condition. "We can speak as you wash or wait until you are done, at your discretion."

Determined to not show any weakness, Tarben decided to take the man up on his offer as if it were Tarben's due to be catered to. He strode to the table. "What is there to talk about? I have my father's emissary to negotiate the treaty. I'm only a warrior and ill-suited to such a task." He took off his leather breastplate and belt, dropping them and his sword to the plush rug floor of the tent. Although he'd kept his weapon and no one had challenged his right to, he wanted to demonstrate that he felt no fear of needing it now. The surroundings were unlike anything he'd ever seen in an encampment. These Moorcondians lived decadent lives.

Soren poured two glasses of wine, setting one beside the wash basin. "No potion has been added, rest assured, if for no other reason that I'm not concerned about your getting sleep any time soon. And I am equally unqualified for such diplomatic negotiations." Sitting in a nearby chair, he took a sip from his cup. "I'm referring to the marriage contract that you and I need to hammer out. And it's best done without Ronan interjecting his view. His feelings on these matters may be somewhat clouded."

In the process of pulling off his tunic, Tarben froze. "What are you talking about? I know nothing of a 'marriage contract'."

"It is the agreement between you, as Ronan's husband, and me, as a representative of his family, as to how you will treat both him and his property."

Tarben yanked the tunic off and tossed it aside. "I will treat him well as he is entitled to as my jarlina, and I care nothing about his property...whatever that might be." Dipping his cupped hands into the water, he splashed some on his face. He was surprised to find that it had been heated. Not quite as bracing as river water, but a delightful surprise, nevertheless.

"This is a standard practice in Moorcondia, especially when a woman is marrying into a higher class."

Picking up the pot of soap, Tarben sniffed before lathering one of the small towels with it. "Ronan is not a woman, and as we are both sons of a king, we are of the same 'class', if I understand your meaning of the term correctly." He started with his neck, determined to go to his wife's side with all the grime of their journey washed away.

"Yes, yes." The Moorcondian prince showed the first signs of testiness. "Notwithstanding those facts, the circumstances are analogous, given that Ronan has obviously submitted himself to your authority and will be living in your country, not his."

Both of those points made Tarben's heart swell, but he was careful not to show it. "What would you have me agree to?" The scent of the soap was pleasant, yet not flowery. He didn't hesitate to substitute his masculine musk for it. When Soren opened his mouth,

Tarben stopped him from answering. "It doesn't matter. Write whatever you want, and I will sign it."

"The terms will be perfectly reasonable — guarantees of visitations to his family each year, acknowledging that as he'll almost certainly die without issue, his property will then go to his younger sister... Ah, here is the scribe now."

An older man entered, carrying a small, short-legged wooden table, an ink pot, quill and paper. He sat cross-legged on the carpeted floor and looked at Soren. "Your highness, whenever you are ready."

"Excellent. Now, as I was saying —"

"Put whatever you want in it and I will sign," Tarben repeated before dropping his breaches.

* * * *

Something was tickling his nose. Tarben batted at it, then opened his eyes when he realized it was his wife's hair. He found the boy wrapped in his arms, his face pressed against Tarben's chest. He was very glad at that moment that he'd washed before lying down beside him. And as they were both naked and aroused, he did the natural thing and rolled them onto their sides. He took the hard cocks in one hand and jerked them to completion within seconds, not caring that he was sullying Prince Soren's pallet. The man had plenty of servants and bedding, from what he'd seen.

Ronan moaned and stretched in his embrace. "That was a lovely way to awaken." Tipping his head back to look at Tarben, he added, "Did my uncle drug me?"

"Yes." It still irked him that the man had taken such appalling liberties, but he couldn't deny that Ronan appeared more rested than he'd seen him on their entire journey together, both up the mountain and down. *Was he ever truly relaxed while in the Dark Mountains?*

Ronan laid his head back down in the crook of Tarben's arms. "Sneaky. How goes the treaty?"

Hearing stress in his wife's voice, Tarben was quick to allay any fears. "It goes well." Not that he actually knew. After signing his name to the marriage contract, he'd joined Ronan immediately. It was a fair assumption, however. "Your uncle has already provided provisions for my men to take to the nearest villages. I have no doubt his actions are saving lives this night."

"He is a good man. Did anything else happen while I slept the day away?"

Tarben stroked his wife's back, enjoying the brief respite from their troubles and hoping that this would be the start of a happier future. "Only that your uncle insisted on drawing up this so-called marriage contract. Our copy of it is over on the table."

Ronan lifted his head to see before lying back down again. "Of course, I should have guessed. I hope he wasn't too tedious or insulting in the negotiations."

"Not at all, mostly because there were none. I told him to put down whatever terms he wished, then I signed it."

Ronan gasped and sat up, his beautiful face still flushed from their brief love-making. The sight of him made Tarben want to do it all over again—and again after that. When he reached for him, however, Ronan batted his hand away. "Stop that! This is important. How could you sign without understanding what you were agreeing to?"

Tarben shrugged. "There was something about allowing you to visit your family, which I intended to do anyway, so long as I accompanied you — purely to ensure your safety during the journey, of course."

"I wouldn't go without you, anyway. I want you to meet and spend time with my family. They'll love you," he added with a smile.

"I would like that to be so, but your love is all I need."

Ronan blushed and dropped his gaze. "I'm still not used to hearing that."

"Then I shall be sure to say often so that you do."

Ronan ran his fingertips down Tarben's chest. "That may prove impossible, but let us both try. Oh," he added after a moment of silence. "What about my property?"

Tarben shrugged again. "I don't know, something about your sister…"

"Well, naturally, if I die without issue, it would all normally go to her because my brother has plenty of his own and will have even more when he becomes king. But you're my husband. You're entitled to some of it, too."

"I don't want it."

"How can you say that? I own a small castle and five villages."

Amused at his wife's ire on his behalf, he was tempted to laugh. But while he hadn't been married long, he knew that would be a bad choice. "That is a great deal, indeed. I still have no desire to lay claim to any of it. You're all that I want." Palming his once-again erect dick, he added, "Always, apparently."

"Oh, you!"

"I understand now why your uncle wanted to keep you from the negotiation. You would have given me too much."

"And you didn't demand enough."

"Ronan, it is done. Your uncle and I have signed both copies. And I could not be happier." As he contemplated soothing his wife's irritation in the time-honored way, his stomach growled, reminding him that they had both eaten little on the ride down. "I smell food. We should eat."

"It's on the table." His wife was still grumpy.

"Then I shall fetch it for you." Tarben rolled off the pallet and got to his feet. There appeared to be a veritable feast for them. It would be good to be able to stuff Ronan after having to ration food. His wife's next words stopped him in his tracks.

"Tarben, after we eat, I want us to get married."

* * * *

Ronan reached for Tarben's hand as they approached the priest his uncle had found. "Thank you for doing this."

Tarben squeezed his hand before answering. "Whatever you want, my love, that is in my power to give you shall be yours."

"It's just that I want to make sure our marriage is truly recognized under the laws of my people." The idea had popped into his head during that infuriating conversation in which he had learned that his husband hadn't pursued his own rights in the marriage contract. And while he understood that this Dark Mountains man really cared nothing about Ronan's property, it did highlight how their marriage had occurred under unusual circumstances, to say the least. Taking their vows the Moorcondian way would solve that problem. His Uncle Soren hadn't seemed surprised at the request, either, and with the treaty already hammered out, signed and sealed, this was the perfect occasion to have the ceremony.

So here they stood in borrowed clothes on Moorcondian land, yet right across the river in order for Tarben's warriors to witness the event. The mood was almost jovial, given the relief that the war had been averted and everyone was getting what they wanted. It wasn't exactly a celebration, not with people still at risk of starvation and the natural distrust and previous animosity simmering under the surface, but Ronan couldn't help being joyful as he and Tarben approached the priest and bowed their heads as the man began to recite the words that the gods apparently wanted to hear. They didn't matter to Ronan, nor did his own when he was prompted to say them. No, it was Tarben's vows that made his heart soar and lungs nearly freeze with unbridled joy. And when they slipped gold bands on each other's fingers — ill-fitting and donated by the gods' knew whom — for the first time, he could truly say *I am married.*

"The gods this day join these two people in marriage," the priest intoned. "Let no mortal tear them apart. Jarl Tarben, you may kiss your…*bride.*"

Neither the priest's discomfort nor the silence of those around him bothered Ronan in the least. All that mattered was the look in his husband's eyes as he gathered him in his arms and claimed his mouth. Ronan clung to him and reveled in how Tarben lifted him off his feet to seal their lips and tongues more tightly. By the time the man let him go again, a groundswell of cheering filled the air. The noise started on the Dark Mountains side, but soon the Moorcondian soldiers joined in.

Best of all, Soren came up and clapped Tarben on the shoulder. "Welcome to the family."

The rest was a blur as he and Tarben walked back to Soren's tent, hand-in-hand. There was no feast because of the scarcity of food, nor did Ronan want one. Even if they could justify such excess instead of sending the food over the border, Ronan didn't want to sit among the others. He craved time alone with his husband. There was one more formality that mattered to him. Despite having given himself to Tarben already, it was important for their Moorcondian marriage to be consummated, as well. It wasn't a matter of the law, but of his heart. Silly as it might seem, the symbolism was important to him. Besides, being fucked by Tarben was fun.

Tugging Tarben toward Soren's table, he let go of the man's hand to grab the bottle of wine. This was one thing that wasn't part of the treaty, because it wasn't considered food. He filled the two glasses and handed one to his husband. "It is a Moorcondian custom to raise a glass of wine in honor of the married couple."

"You seem to have a lot of customs, wife, but this is one that I can support." He started to drink, then said, "Does it count if we do it for ourselves?"

"I think under the circumstances, it does." Ronan took a few sips before putting his glass down. He wanted a clear head for the night to come. He grabbed a small bottle at the same time he plucked the empty glass from Tarben's fingers. "Now, take me to bed."

Tarben didn't need to be told twice. Scooping Ronan up into his arms, he strode toward the pallet. "What have you there?"

"Oil. It's probably not as good as Fren's cream, but it will get the job done."

Tarben's nostrils flared. "I love how you think ahead, wife." He gave Ronan a smacking kiss before lowering him to his feet.

It didn't take long for Ronan to find himself naked and straddling his husband's equally bare body. Their erections brushed against each other and Tarben clasped them together in his large fist. Ronan threw his head back and moaned. "I love what your touch does to me."

"Then let me make you even happier."

Ronan opened his eyes and stayed Tarben's hand with his own. "No, not like that. I want you inside me."

Tarben's expression turned almost feral. "You don't have to ask twice." He reached for the bottle of oil and poured a generous amount onto his dick.

Ronan watched avidly as his husband's cock turned shiny. He knew a passing regret that he hadn't taken the man into his mouth beforehand. He was getting pretty good at cocksucking, although unable to take much of Tarben's large dick, and was somewhat surprised by how much he enjoyed the practice. And there would be plenty of time to continue to do so—the whole rest of their lives, in fact. Then his thoughts flew out of his head as Tarben began the process of opening him.

The man was maddeningly slow about it, using only one finger at first to invade his hole. The slow fucking Tarben gave him with it caused his arousal to grow but again at an irksome pace. Closing his eyes, Ronan rocked into the invasion, forcing his body to relax to demonstrate how quickly he could become ready to take his husband's dick. The effort worked—as one finger became two and two turned into three. He moaned and squeezed each time Tarben pulled back. He curled his fingers against his thighs, and his breaths stuttered out as his arousal grew. He was afraid he would come too soon, so he clamped the base of his own shaft to stop himself.

"Please, Tarben. Please fuck me, now and *hard*."

"How can I refuse." Tarben's voice was strained and thick with passion. But when he tried to lift Ronan up to sit on his cock, Ronan twisted away and rolled to his side.

He grabbed Tarben's waist, trying to turn him around. Of course, it was like moving one of the Dark Mountains, so he had to make his intent clear. "I want you to mount me with me on my back. I love having you take control." The first time, he'd ridden his husband only because of the man's injury. With that healed enough, Ronan felt confident in his selfishness.

Tarben didn't question the plea. Instead, he rolled between Ronan's legs and nudged them farther apart. His slick cock butted against Ronan's ass, seeking and finding his hole. It entered him with all the force of Tarben's mastery behind it. Ronan threw his head back and moaned as he was stretched and filled. How was it possible that even discomfort made him shudder with desire? Being covered by Tarben's large body, Ronan found the fulfillment of his dreams. This was what he had always wanted—for a strong man to take command of him, control his body while protecting it with all his strength and showering him with love. He quivered under the assault, breathily urging his husband to do more.

Ronan got his wish when Tarben lifted one of Ronan's legs up and over his shoulder. It allowed him to thrust deeper into Ronan's channel while pegging the sensitive part of him with more vigor. Ronan cried out as his climax crashed over him. He squeezed Tarben's shaft as hard as he could, determined to bring him over the edge, too. His husband's shout was loud enough that it might have brought all the soldiers in camp running. But Ronan didn't care. It told him he'd done his duty, brought pleasure to his husband and in turn to himself. This had been his destiny all along.

When they stopped shuddering from the aftershocks of their orgasms, Tarben carefully pulled out of Ronan's ass. He clenched the dick, trying to keep it in place, but he was no match for Tarben's power. He never would be, which was how he wanted it, even when it meant not getting his way. It was silly anyway, because Tarben returned quickly with a wet cloth to clean him up and a glass of wine for them to share. Ronan took the offered sips with his head snuggled into the crook of the man's arm. He should have been sleepy, but after his drug-induced nap he felt wide awake, his mind turning.

Tarben patted his ass. "What are you thinking about, my love?"

"I was thinking about Tanulf, actually."

Tarben stiffened. "Why? Is the memory of what he did making you afraid of my touch?"

"No!" Ronan raised his head to look his husband in the eye. "Never worry about that. You complete me in every way. No one has ever made me happier, and nothing can change that." He pecked him on the lips to accent his point. "It had just occurred to me that if he hadn't set his horrid plan into motion, we would never have met. Given all the misery he caused, it's hard to believe this but…I wonder if the gods had a hand in it. Only they could have truly known what was in my heart and how impossible it was for me to fulfill it."

Draining the glass of wine, Tarben put it aside before pulling Ronan on top of him so that their bodies lay flush against each other and their foreheads touched. "I cannot say whether your gods or the All Mother conspired to bring us together. What I do know," he added, his eyes getting moist, "right down to the deepest part of my bones, is that I would have always found you."

Ronan sniffed back his own tears. "And that's what I always hoped, that a man would find me…and keep me. I am yours." He'd said it before and would continue to say it for the rest of their lives. He, Prince Ronan of Moorcondia, had finally achieved his destiny — as a treaty bride with the Dark Mountains.

Want to see more from this author?
Here's a taster for you to enjoy!

His Harem: Room for Elijah
Samantha Cayto

Excerpt

Elijah walked into the club, blinking a bit owlishly at the change from the waning brightness outside to the dim lighting. It was early still, so the place wasn't packed, although there was a big group of girls crowded around the tables by the stage. They looked as if they'd started partying early, and it was clearly a bachelorette party, given that one of them wore a tacky wedding veil. He had to step to one side as a couple of guys strode in, supremely confident and laughing as they held hands. He took a moment to appreciate how amazing the sight was. Here in Boston, guys could do that, and while they likely still got hassled, he doubted it was anything like the shunning and hostility he would have gotten back home.

"Sorry, kid. This is a twenty-one and older club."

Elijah started at the deep male voice coming from behind the bar. He made his feet turn toward it instead of running out. The man standing there was tall enough that Elijah had to crane his neck some to stare him in the face. And, oh God, it was a handsome one! It was the kind of fantasy man his rural and unsophisticated mind dared to dream of. It was like staring at an action figure, all broad muscles, shown off by a tight, black T-shirt, and there was a close-cropped beard hugging his face. It was nothing like the facial hair of men he'd grown up with. This wasn't a 'mountain man, salt-of-the-Earth' type. It was more like 'I forgot to shave for a few days', and it highlighted his strong, square jaw. The lines around the guy's eyes pegged him somewhere in the thirty- to forty-year-old range, exactly what Elijah found attractive. The man's hair was jet black and not much longer than the beard. But his eyes were a bright blue and gazing at him as if he were waiting for something.

Oh, right. He's asking about my age. Hitching his backpack higher on his shoulder, Elijah tried to appear more confident than he felt. "I'm not here to drink. I was just hoping maybe you had some odd jobs that I could do?" His voice sort of squeaked at the end, and he could feel his face heating with embarrassment.

The man studied him for a few uncomfortable seconds. "Did you just get off the train at South Station?"

"Um, no. A bus, actually." Lots of them, because it wasn't a straight shot from his slow town in nowhere Pennsylvania to the comparatively bright lights of the City of Boston. He knew he looked pretty grungy, having assessed himself in the public restroom before legging it from the station. He'd washed up a little, ignoring the startled and somewhat too-interested stares from the other occupants, so he knew he was relatively presentable.

The older man leaned his elbows on the bar and stared a while longer before saying, "I bet you spent most of the money you had getting here."

Even more embarrassed now, Elijah dropped his gaze. "Yes, sir." He raised it again and straightened his shoulders. "That's why I need a job." He glanced around the large room. "I don't drink, like *ever*, so you don't have to worry about my stealing alcohol. Is it illegal for me to work here?"

The man shook his head and his lips turned up. "Nope. It's not even illegal for you to be a patron, so long as you aren't drinking alcohol. It's just my policy to keep the under twenty-ones out. Boston is a big college town, and kids are very good at getting fake IDs. I'm not willing to risk my liquor license by letting them even think they can get in here." He cocked his head. "Are you looking to perform?"

"Perform?" The meaning of the question was still forming in his head when the music dimmed, and a loud voice boomed.

"Ladies and gentlemen, let's get the evening started. Please welcome to the stage our one and only Vanna Van Dyke!"

The room erupted into raucous applause. Elijah turned to watch with open-mouthed amazement as a woman strutted out from the wings of the stage. No, a *queen*. He knew that's who he was watching, because that was the whole point of this club called *Queens*. The website said the place was a combination of Irish pub and cabaret, featuring the best in drag entertainment. The tall, pale blonde swayed her hips across the stage, blowing kisses to an adoring crowd. She was clearly a favorite, and the way she wore the skin-tight, shimmering gown, one couldn't see anything masculine about her. She was the epitome of a sexy female, from the top of her towering head of curls to her fuck-me stilettos. And when she started lip-syncing her first Taylor Swift song, Elijah became enthralled.

"Are you hungry?"

The unexpected question jarred Elijah back to his reality. Forcing his gaze away from the performance, he looked back at the man. "Yes, sir." He hated admitting it, but there wasn't enough left in his wallet to pay for much. "I don't think I can afford to eat here, though."

The man straightened and pointed to the nearest bar stool. "Park your butt there, don't even think about reaching for any of the bottles and I'll get you a cheeseburger…on the house," he added.

Elijah's stomach rumbled at the offer, but honesty and fairness had been ingrained in him all his life. He might not be the straight boy his family demanded, but he had morals, nevertheless. "Thanks. I don't want you to get into trouble with your boss, though. I doubt he likes your giving away food."

The man chuckled. "No worries, kid. I'm Dermott McCarthy, and this is my place. I *am* the boss," he added for emphasis. "I think I can swing a free burger, and after you eat, we can talk about what kind of work you might do around here."

Elijah was too elated to object. He dutifully sat where indicated, putting his backpack on the floor between his legs. "Thank you, sir. I appreciate it."

The man shot him a look that was hard to read, except all he could think of was *hungry.* "I like the 'sir', but you can call me Dermott. And," he added with a serious expression, "just so we're clear, I'm not looking for anything more than a little hard work for mostly crappy pay. No other service will be required of you. Understand?"

Elijah nodded, unable to say anything past the sudden lump in his throat. When he'd left home, he'd known full well what LGBTQI kids often had to do to survive on their own. It was possible that this man, Dermott, was simply laying a trap. Except he seemed sincere, and Elijah desperately wanted to believe that he'd landed in a relatively safe place. Time would tell, and in the meantime, he'd enjoy the meal and the show. When Dermott walked toward the other end of the bar, Elijah turned back to the stage. Vanna Van Dyke was on song number two, and the audience was already showering her with money. It gave him thoughts of trying drag himself. Then he shut them down quickly. There was no way he could ever perform in front of an audience, but that didn't mean he couldn't enjoy watching others. For the first time in days, he felt the tension draining from his body. Things might turn out okay after all.

* * * *

"Hey, Daddy!"

Elijah had already scarfed down the delicious cheeseburger and was working his way through a mound of fries when Vanna hopped onto the stool next to him. Dermott was still tending the bar, and he greeted Vanna with a broad smile and smacking kiss that left Elijah gawking. While he'd managed to catch some TV shows where guys had kissed other guys, he'd never seen it up close and in person. The sight of the naked affection between the two men did funny things to his insides. Vanna might look like a woman, but he knew underneath it all, she was a he. At least he thought so. He could be wrong about that. Maybe Vanna was trans, something that his family had disavowed as against God's will. Given his own experiences with being 'different', Elijah couldn't bring himself to condemn things beyond his experience.

Vanna slapped a wad of bills on the bar top. "It's a good crowd, even this early. Do I have enough to buy a beer?" The queen fluttered her lashes at Dermott.

The man rolled his eyes and put a glass of soda water with a slice of lime in front of the performer. "Not for another year, as you well know. And I still haven't decided if I'm going to let you drink, even then."

Vanna wrapped bright red lips around the straw and took a deep pull of the water before saying, "You're so mean, Daddy." The tone was a teasing one, flirtatious even.

"A brat like you needs rules." Dermott didn't seem at all insulted. He stared into Vanna's eyes with such obvious affection that Elijah had to look away.

Vanna waved his thumb in Elijah's direction. "How about him? He doesn't look twenty-one."

"That's because he's not, and he's drinking Coke, no rum included." Dermott moved away to serve another customer.

After a few more sips, Vanna turned wide, heavily made-up eyes toward Elijah. "Hi. You're new."

Elijah wasn't sure how to respond. Swallowing his food, he forced himself to meet the queen head-on. Her eyes were an even brighter shade of blue than Dermott's. This close, he could see that her makeup was more elaborate and exaggerating than anything he'd ever seen before — not that the women of his family ever wore any. The elder women had always condemned it as sinful, as had their church — just one more thing he'd silently disagreed with. The contouring and shading of Vanna's face gave an illusion of it being more feminine than it probably was, although Vanna was drop-dead gorgeous by any standard. Elijah was fascinated at how little it took to make the transformation.

Not wanting to be rude, he looked away. "I'm Elijah. I just arrived in Boston and was looking for work."

"Oh, mama, you've come to the right place." Vanna leaned over some. "You have great bone structure. And you're so petite. Men are going to lap you up with a spoon."

Before Elijah could form a response, Dermott returned. "Easy, baby. The kid literally just got off the bus, and he's not here to learn how to be a queen. Are you?" He trained his eyes on Elijah.

He could feel another blush coming on. "No, sir. I don't want to be an entertainer. I couldn't be as good as anyone here, anyway." His glanced at the stage, where another queen was prancing to Tina Turner in sky-high heels. The queen was as impressive as Vanna had been, although this one was darker all around and was wearing a corset cinched impossibly tight. Her hair was a mass of ropey curls that shook as if they had a life of their own.

Vanna giggled. "That's what Medusa said when she first arrived. Remember? And look at her now!" Vanna leaned over toward Elijah again and said, "She can corset her waist to nineteen inches. Can you believe it? Scarlett O'Hara would be green with envy."

Elijah shook his head, understanding that he was supposed to be impressed. And he was, but he was also starting to think he'd made a mistake. This world had always appealed to him when he'd caught glimpses of it on TV and the Internet. Now that he was wading into it, his insecurities flared, and he wasn't sure this was where he belonged at all. His conservative, rural upbringing hadn't prepared him for the intensity of the attention he was getting—nor was he able to handle the emotional and physical reactions he was having toward Dermott and, surprisingly, Vanna. Although virile men had always been his go-to fantasy, it was weird how attracted he was to someone so overtly female. Girls had never interested him. And he'd always been careful to hide his erections and was stingy with his own hand. Right at the moment, however, he craved somewhere private where he could take care of his disconcerting arousal.

But he had made a bargain, sort of, with Dermott. He owed the man labor for the meal, and he wasn't one to run out on an obligation. Wiping his mouth with his napkin, he slid off the stool and grabbed his plate and empty glass. "What can I do to help, sir?"

By way of answer, Dermott pulled an apron and plastic tub out from under the counter and placed them in front of him. "You can start by bussing your own stuff, then go clear that table in the corner."

"Yes, sir." Putting his plate and glass into the tub, he got to work.

About the Author

Samantha Cayto is a Boston-area native who practices as a business lawyer by day while writing erotic romance at night—the steamier the better. She likes to push the envelope when it comes to writing about passion and is delighted other women agree that guy-on-guy sex is the hottest ever.

She lives a typical suburban life with her husband, three kids and four dogs. Her children don't understand why they can't read what she writes, but her husband is always willing to lend her a hand—and anything else—when she needs to choreograph a scene.

Samantha loves to hear from readers. You can find her contact information, website details and author profile page at https://www.pride-publishing.com

PUBLISHING

Sign up for our newsletter and find out about all our romance book releases, eBook sales and promotions, sneak peeks and FREE romance books!